Praise for Linda Dorre

"Dorrell ably weaves these perso
story of Southern racial strife, depicting interracial friendships
as early, faltering attempts at repairing the breech rather than
easy solutions to centuries of oppression. . . . Her characters are
emotionally authentic . . . a delight."

Publishers Weekly

"Historical fiction with a kick and some devious surprises."

Library Journal

"Woven into the fabric of a compelling story are timeless lessons
on the human spirit and the spiritual/emotional resources of the
Christian gospel in the face of physical and cultural obstacles
to establishing loving relationships and nurturing communities
of faith."

Midwest Book Review

"There are so many great things in this book that it's difficult to
narrow it down in a review."

Romantic Times

"A tale of truth, healing, and beauty. . . . Dorrell gives us a
story of rebuilding and redemption that will linger long after
the book is done."

The Grand Rapids Press

"Dorrell's tale is to reading what an afternoon drive is to Sun-
days: relaxing, interesting, enjoyable. The author's characters
are well-developed, and many readers will empathize with them
on several levels as they deal with dominating family members
and the injustice of prejudice."

Christian Retailing

"A compelling story . . . with tensions and struggles simmering through the pages. Ms. Dorrell follows in the mighty footsteps of Southern writers such as Eudora Welty, Flannery O'Connor, and Harper Lee and does a good job keeping up the pace."

This Christian Life (www.thischristianlife.com)

"Evokes the racial passions of a South Carolina town that will never be the same as an old church comes to new life."

Bookviews' "Pick of the Month" on www.Bookviews.com

Praise for Linda Dorrell's *Face to Face*

"A tragic suspenseful story of love: the love of a mother and her daughter, and the love between husbands and wives, God and his children. . . . *Face to Face* is a good read. [Linda Dorrell] creates strong characters and sends us on a trail of intrigue, faith, hope, and love. When you pick up *Face to Face* be prepared to read all the way through, as you won't want to put it down until the wow ending. If you love suspense, true crime, and stories of hope, *Face to Face* is a must have."

The Word on Romance

"Readers will feel the heroine's anxiety and struggles as she searches for her daughter in this bittersweet story."

Romantic Times

"[A] powerful and emotionally moving saga of the search for redemption and second chances."

Midwest Book Review

"The unexpected ending admirably avoids an easy conclusion."

Publishers Weekly

THE TREES
OF EDEN

A NOVEL

LINDA DORRELL

Fleming H. Revell
A Division of Baker Book House Co
Grand Rapids, Michigan 49516

© 2004 by Linda Dorrell

Published by Fleming H. Revell
a division of Baker Book House Company
P.O. Box 6287, Grand Rapids, MI 49516-6287
www.bakerbooks.com

Printed in the United States of America

Library of Congress Cataloging-in-Publication Data
Dorrell, Linda.
   The trees of Eden : a novel / Linda Dorrell.
     p.   cm.
   ISBN 0-8007-5920-6 (pbk.)
   1. Girls—Fiction. 2. Mothers and daughters—Fiction. 3. Conflict of generations—Fiction. 4. South Carolina—Fiction I. Title.
PS3604.077T69 2004
813'.6—dc22   2003018366

Scripture is taken from the King James Version of the Bible.

Spirituals on pages 32, 35, 60, and 122 are taken from: Federal Writers Project, South Carolina, *Twenty-one Negro Spirituals,* Viking Press (1937), http://newdeal.feri.org/fwp/fwp05.htm. New Deal Network, http://newdeal.feri.org (October 27, 2001).

For all the strong women
of the Dorrell and Meekins families,
past, present, and future

THE CHARACTERS

Wren Birdsong, seventeen years old

Huldah Birdsong, her mother

Mallon Birdsong, her father

Wren's brothers: Charley, Theodore, Wilson, Micah, Nehemiah, Jeremiah

Mim (Mrs. McRae), Wren's maternal grandmother

Dr. Seymour McRae, Huldah Birdsong's deceased father

Odessa and Pandora, freed family slaves who live with Mim

Miss Elaine "Lanie" Lansdale, headmistress of Miss Lansdale's Academy for Young Ladies

Frederick McRae, Wren's uncle from San Francisco

Thracia Mills

Sloan "Skeeter" Lowe

Mrs. Lapis Cochrane, owner of the milliner's shop in Bethel Creek

Jason Spurley, an Army inductee

Rev. Jonas John McKechnie, minister of the First Presbyterian Church

Dr. Connell Redmond, a physician with the United States Public Health Service

Mr. Derwin, undertaker

THE ANIMALS

Tiberius and Titania, orange marmalade cats

Pegasus, Wren's horse

Jake, the mule

Saturn, Theodore's horse

Neptune, Wilson's horse

CONTENTS

To every thing there is a season, and a time to every purpose under the heaven: A time to be born, and a time to die; a time to plant, and a time to pluck up that which is planted.

Ecclesiastes 3:1–2

1

BOILING WATERMELONS

Some folks spend their lives asking questions no one on earth can answer.

What will happen today? Next week? Next year? Will I get married? Will I have children? What will they grow up to be? Why are some people so awful and have everything go right, while others are wonderful and have everything go wrong?

I was contemplating these deep philosophical thoughts as I dangled my feet in the cool flowing waters of Bethel Creek. Trickling water tickled my toes like sprigs of new spring grass.

Foot dangling and pondering life's mysteries were among my few pleasures in a reality marked by incessant responsibilities, tiring burdens, and unending chores. Little did I know, that hot September afternoon in 1918 when I was called upon by my mother, Mrs. Huldah Birdsong, to see to Miss Picklemeyer's infirmities, that in a short while I would confront questions I would never have thought to ask in a thousand lifetimes.

Of course I didn't know about Miss Picklemeyer. I just heard Mother hollering for me to get myself up to the house or I'd find myself doing not only my chores but those of my six brothers as well. That wouldn't have been unusual because I usually wound up doing all their work and mine anyway. Boys always seem to get away with everything. Me, I couldn't take five minutes to enjoy a little refreshment for my soul on a steamy afternoon if I tried.

"Wren Birdsong!" Mother's shouting scattered birds from the trees, and not a few forest animals decided life might be more peaceful on the other side of the creek. "Time, child! You are taking too much time!" The volume and detail of Mother's tirade grew with each passing moment. I sighed and pulled my feet from the current, drying them on the cool grass, tearing my mind away from my next planned topic—pleasant reveries of life beyond Bethel Creek—before snatching my stockings and making a run up the embankment.

"I'm coming," I muttered, not willing to give her another piece of myself one moment sooner than necessary. Grabbing spindly pine saplings for balance, I made it to the bluff, where our farmhouse overlooked the creek basin with large open windows that watched over it like haughty eyes.

Mother sat in our surrey, wearing her usual black dress and a wide-brimmed straw hat adorned with a gigantic bow that stuck out on either side, making her look as if she had grown two elephant ears that flapped in the hot breeze.

"Wren Birdsong, one of our neighbors is in need of our help. When I call you I expect you to be at hand within moments," she began as I climbed into the surrey. She shook the reins, and Jake, the old mule, flicked his ears and broke into an uncharacteristically brisk trot, probably fearing that she would reprimand him next if he didn't hop to. "Folks depend on me, and I need your help. If you've got any interest at all in following in my footsteps, then you'd better get a move on from now on."

"I'm not becoming a doctor, Mother," I replied matter-of-factly, or so I thought. "I already told you: I'm planning to become a suffragette."

She began laughing and quaking so that Jake nearly skewed us off the road. Steadying him, she shook her head. "Wren, you know those suffragettes are nothing but a bunch of dissatisfied rich ladies who don't know a woman's place is home with her children, serving her own kith and kin, instead of running around in the streets, getting those white dresses mussed, and showing themselves to be the immoral heathens they are."

I sighed and commenced putting on my stockings, a challenge with that surrey scooting every which way. "Mother, our country gave the right to vote to the Negroes last century. If they can pass the test, they can vote. I believe women have a God-given right to the same privileges." I raised up and watched a blackbird pecking at an ungleaned ear of corn in Mr. Flagler's field as we passed.

My formal education had ended the previous May when I was graduated from Miss Lansdale's Academy for Young Ladies in the nearby village of Bethel Creek. Mother and Papa believed all children should have a proper education, and, seeing as how I was the only girl in a passel of boys, they thought I needed to be among my own kind.

At the florescent age of eleven, I was placed under the academy's direction.

It turns out I received more education than they bargained for. I suppose they thought the academy would school me in the refined arts—arts that would help me get a husband, someone who would support me and take me from under their wizened care.

They didn't bargain on Miss Lanie Lansdale.

Miss Lansdale was quite progressive. Self-styled after one of Charles Dana Gibson's magazine portraits, she was Rutledge County's own Gibson Girl. Beautifully coiffed, elegantly attired, she turned heads and swept through the streets as if she were a one-woman Fourth of July parade, be it January or October. Her looks were a clever cover for all the brainpower she disguised with a suffusive charm that made even the dourest codger break a smile.

Regarding education, Mother had her limits. She had no use for stuffy, arrogant professors—which Miss Lanie most definitely was not—nor anyone who didn't have sense enough to tell the month of June from a june bug. And although my parents believed that knowledge learned from books had its place—goodness knows, they filled our house with volumes on every subject imaginable—they also believed books were no substitute for life's classrooms, the tactile world of experience.

We girls worshiped Miss Lanie. She idealized everything we wanted to be—witty, intelligent, adventurous. When she wasn't running the academy, she toured the United States and boarded ships to mysterious foreign lands. Rumor had it that Miss Lanie's parents were among the wealthiest citizens of some city up North and upon their death, Miss Lanie had taken her inheritance, pitched the stuffiness of the big city, and removed herself to Bethel to enjoy the climate and, as she put it, "do some real good for those who need it most."

So along with herself, she imported the idea of women's suffrage, which I latched on to with all ten fingers and all ten toes. But the day I finished high school was the day my real education began, under the sometimes disorienting, intimidating, frustrating, but always fascinating, tutelage of Mrs. Huldah McRae Birdsong.

"Child, what are you thinking about?" Mother regarded me with a sideways look.

"Miss Lanie."

Mother rolled her eyes. "I don't know what your father and I were thinking, sending you to be educated by that woman," she said as the cotton fields, growing pregnant with bolls, rolled by. We were approaching Miss Picklemeyer's house, which sat on the outskirts of town. I could already hear her crying out in German. I had only studied French and Latin, so I couldn't understand what she was saying, although it sounded like a plea of some sort.

Miss Picklemeyer was on her back, flailing about the watermelon patch like a topsy-turvy turtle. Two neighbor boys stood there, watching her thrash among the last of the ripening watermelons. She grew them to sell at the local store and sometimes sold them from her front yard. Seeing all those melons put me in mind of a story Papa once told about how he picked a watermelon on a steamy day, sliced it open, and found the juices boiling inside.

"Getting scalded by a watermelon," he said, rubbing his ear. "That's one thing you'll never forget if you live to be a hundred."

Mother and I got out of the surrey and went over to Miss Picklemeyer, who stopped her flailing and became rather peaceful. She was quite flushed, whether from the sun or flailing I'm not sure. Mother put her hand on her chin and assessed the situation, then pointed to the boys, who were snickering behind their hands.

"Did it occur to you two that maybe she just needed some help to get up?"

The boys laughed louder and ran behind a row of camellias that lined the yard. I could see their feet below the foliage and hear their whispers.

"You help me up, Miss Huldah?" Miss Picklemeyer spoke quietly, having never shed her German accent. Her father had emigrated to the United States when she was a child of eight; however, her accent was ingrained by then, and so was her father's wish that she maintain evidence of her heritage in spite of his move.

Mother indicated that I should take one of Miss Picklemeyer's arms. I could barely get both my hands around it. Mother grabbed her on the other side, and we commenced pulling Miss Picklemeyer to her feet. After many grunts, groans, moans, and other assorted exclamations, on her part and ours, we managed to stand the woman up and walk her to a nearby bench, where she rested and caught her breath. I sagged beneath a peach tree, longing for the creek's cooling relief, as I watched Mother examine Miss Picklemeyer.

I often accompanied Mother as she saw to the infirmities of the citizens of Bethel Creek. The nearest physician worked in a town twenty miles away. He was frequently too ill himself to make the sometimes treacherous journey into the pinewoods and swamps that typified our county. The military had drafted most of the state's physicians into war service, so there was a shortage of trained practitioners to care for the sick and diseased. Mother frequently commented that what we needed in Bethel Creek was a young physician who could tame Miss Lanie, purge her of her worldly ways, and keep our populace well and tended to at the same time. Mother slapped a hand across Miss Picklemeyer's forehead and quickly drew it away.

"You're feverish," she pronounced to Miss Picklemeyer as she dug through her bag for one of her fever remedies. "Mother, it's two hundred degrees out here," I said, fanning myself with my hat. "How can you tell?" The question popped out, though I knew better. Mother preferred not to use a thermometer, claiming the back of her hand was just as accurate. She proved this on several occasions when I had questioned her authority. One thing I found out early on was that you never questioned Huldah Birdsong's authority on anything, unless you were willing to suffer the consequences.

"When you've been doing this as long as I have, daughter, you can tell." She motioned me over, and I reluctantly gave up my patch of shade. Taking my hand, she placed it first against Miss Picklemeyer's forehead, then her cheek. Her face did have a different feel from one that is simply hot from too much time in the sun. "Help me get her inside."

Miss Picklemeyer could barely walk. It was all the two of us could do just to get her up the three steps to the front door, then inside and down the hall to the daybed in the parlor. "Do you notice her color, Wren?"

We laid the woman down, and I observed her while Mother went to the kitchen and filled the basin with cool water. "She looks a little blue," I said when Mother returned. Taking the basin and a rag, I began bathing Miss Picklemeyer's face and arms. "And listen to how she's breathing."

Mother leaned down and placed her head against Miss Picklemeyer's chest. Raising her head, she nodded. "Pneumonia," she pronounced and commenced digging in her bag again.

From the time I could toddle across the yard, the contents of Mother's black bag had fascinated me. It was just like the one real doctors carry and was filled with all manner of ointments and salves, tonics and elixirs, concoctions aimed at either curing what ailed you, making you comfortable if a cure wasn't possible, or simply distracting you with a host of new miseries. Some of these were patent medicines that she purchased from the store in town, or through catalogs, and sometimes traveling salesmen who sought her out in her garden and spent hours giving her their personal medicine show.

Then there were the ones she formulated herself.

Mother was a student of many things, the foremost of these being the Bible, the lattermost being almost anything that grows, either wild or cultivated. I guess you could say her greatest passions other than salvation and service were the plants that grew in Bible times.

Mother plucked a vial from the bag, retrieved a medicine dropper, and began forcing the liquid past Miss Picklemeyer's lips. After a few moments, the old woman's breathing slowed. Mother and I watched as she fell into a fitful sleep.

"Are you sure it's pneumonia?" I continued to regard her breathing as out of character with what I had previously associated with that illness.

"I've seen it a thousand times," Mother said, packing her bag. "Let's go. She'll sleep for a few hours. In the meantime we'll go home and get supper on the table. I'll come back later and spend the night."

"I can come back," I volunteered, looking for any excuse to get out of the house for a night, even if it was to watch a sick old woman.

"No, Wren," Mother replied as we made our way back to the surrey. "You're not sufficiently ready."

Mother still had this idea that I was going to follow her lead and become the community's healer. As we got underway, I renewed my suffragette aspirations.

"I believe I can make far more difference by helping women gain the right to vote than by running around pulling out splinters and bandaging wounds that could be prevented merely by the wounded having been more careful in how they applied their ax or hammer." The shadows had lengthened now, and a slight breeze threw little clouds of dust across the road ahead of Jake. "If women receive the right to vote, we can have a say in matters of national importance."

"What matters might those be?" Mother made no effort to hide the sarcasm.

"Those espoused by the great women's advocates of the past and present," I replied. "Elizabeth Cady Stanton and Susan B. Anthony. And Mrs. Inez Milholland Boissevain can't have died for nothing."

I could see that Mother was trying not to roll her eyeballs. Mrs. Boissevain was a favorite topic of Miss Lanie's, and mine by association. I suppose Mother had been subjected to more information on this heroine of our cause than she cared to know. Mother firmly believed in not cluttering the brain to leave room for matters of true importance—God, medicines, plants, the wisdom of Solomon. At least matters that were important to her.

Presently we arrived at the house to find my brothers outside in the yard engaged in their various interests and pursuits, save Micah, who rarely left the house. Sometimes he would go into the yard, but he hadn't been past the front fence in years, for reasons we could not pry out of him. Mother liked to quote the verse about how we are all fearfully and wonderfully made but that Micah got more of the fearful part.

For my part, I spent as much time as possible trying to ignore all these males who surrounded me daily. Don't get me wrong—I believe men are the equal of women in many ways, but in many ways I find our sex quite superior, and I did not wish to spend the bulk of my time trying to bring them up to my standards of behavior, which is all I seemed to do when I was around them. I trounced into the kitchen and began mixing up a batch of biscuits while Mother stoked the stove until it practically turned red, then put a pot of butter beans on to boil.

One by one my brothers—Charley, Theodore, Wilson, Micah, Nehemiah, and Jeremiah—filed into the kitchen and assumed their places at the long table. Charley, Theodore, and Wilson were older than me, and the other three younger. Why Mother switched to biblical names after my birth was not known to me at the time, although I later discovered that this was when she considered herself truly saved, not by the birth of a daughter, but by her recognition that the Son was the way to true salvation. Apparently, she had lacked in her previous religious training, or had come under the influence of a more evangelical minister who set her right. Mim, my grandmother, her mother, had strange notions about many aspects of life. Superstitions and old wives' tales governed her daily activities, and while she believed in God, her deity was much different from the one my mother invoked. About why I got named for a bird, Mother said it was because a Carolina wren lit on the windowsill the moment after my birth, and she took it as a sign straight from the Lord that Caroline Wren was to be my name. So that's my full given name: Caroline Wren Birdsong.

Mother blamed Mim's beliefs on Odessa and Pandora, two ancient colored women who lived on Mim's place just up the road from ours. Mim's father had once owned Odessa and Pandora, and Mother seemed to think that their continued existence was some sort of curse and that they had somehow possessed Mim with their mixture of Christian beliefs and pagan African heritage. The sisters claimed they were descended from a slave named America, the only slave on the plantation who was sold away after his master died rather than willed to the children and grandchildren as were his own progeny. I often thought about America, what had happened to him, who had owned him next, and why someone had precipitated the cruel joke of naming a chattel slave after a land that symbolized freedom.

I noticed that Mother kept watching the door expectantly, waiting for Papa to come in from wherever it was he had gone that particular day. We kept cooking and soon had a table full of bowls of steaming beans and squash and rice, plates of hot biscuits with jars of homemade scuppernong and huckleberry jelly, and tall pitchers of lemonade that my brothers drank like horses after a hard run across a dusty field.

"Papa is here," she said all of a sudden. She and I sat down, and we all became quiet as she gave the blessing.

"Our Father, who truly art in heaven, we beseech thy many blessings on this food and these children. I pray that thou wilt turn Wren away from her rash idea of becoming a suffragette . . ."

At this, my brothers collectively began to titter. I despised it when Mother would single me out to the Lord, as if I were the only one who had done anything that merited individual attention. I opened my eyes and glared at everyone, futilely.

19

"She knows not what she does, Lord, and fails to seek thy will. We pray thy knowledge and wisdom upon her, that thy grace may shine upon her soul. In the name of thy most precious Son, the Lamb of God. Amen."

Everyone raised their heads and looked at me in unison. I glowered at Mother, who patted my cheek. Resisting the urge to slap her hand away, I began filling my plate.

"Mallon, our daughter has the most outlandish ideas," she began, smearing scuppernong jelly on a biscuit for Jeremiah, who was only six and hadn't quite mastered eating utensils such as knives. "She believes that the good Lord has called her to bring women the right to vote, as if we already don't run everything now, only you men haven't realized it yet."

I covered a mound of rice with butter beans and pot liquor and wondered why it was called that, considering it contained no spirits of any kind and was simply the broth created by the mixture of water and cooked beans. As I began to eat, I decided it was not in my favor now to debate Mother, because I could never convince her to my point of view, no matter how many facts and details I had to bolster my argument. It was to my great relief that she turned her attention to my eldest brother.

"Charles, are you prepared for your journey tomorrow?" she asked, wiping Jeremiah's face.

"Yes, Mother," he answered with a full mouth. "I'm enjoying this meal because I've been assured that food at the camp won't be nearly as wholesome as that which lies before me now."

It pained me no end that Charley was heading off to boot camp, then to the war, which the newspapers so hyperbolically called "The Great War," as if there is any such thing. Along with my views on women's right to vote, I had also become an ardent pacifist. I believed there was nothing great or noble about war, which laid waste to lives and land and only, in my mind, went on to produce more hatred and distrust in the end rather than anything resembling lasting peace. I was constantly reminded of the War of Northern Aggression—Miss Lanie had been taken to task by many townspeople for calling that conflict the Civil War—by aged veterans who had nothing to do but sit on porches, rocking their days away, cherishing their memories of glories long past. This was the twentieth century, and I lived in the United States of America, not the Confederate States. That war was over. It was long past time for folks to quit fighting it.

"I think you should refuse to go on the grounds that you are a conscientious objector," I said, watching my brother's handsome face as he devoured biscuit after biscuit, dripping jelly down his chin as badly as Jeremiah.

"But I don't object, Wren," he said softly, smiling at me from the other end of the table. "I believe we are fighting for a great cause."

"There is no cause great enough for thousands of men in the prime of youth to lose their lives." I put down my fork and folded my hands under my chin. "I believe President Wilson is misguided in his insistence on involving us in the affairs of other nations."

Charley shook his head. "It is a great cause, and one that I am honored to serve."

"Serving for one's beliefs is never dishonorable," Mother said, her eyes sweeping across everyone's plates. "Now finish up, everyone. I must see to Miss Picklemeyer."

"I can clean up, Mother," I volunteered. At least maybe if she left early, I wouldn't have to endure any more uninformed opinions.

"Very well, then. I'll take my leave." She looked toward the end of the table. "Mallon, I leave them under your care."

21

With that she rose from the table after a last swipe at Jeremiah's face, and soon I heard the mule clip off down the lane.

My brothers dispersed, except Charley, who helped me remove the plates to the sink.

"When do you think she'll accept it?" he asked, staring at Father's plate.

"Perhaps never," I said, removing the plate that I had set there every night for three years, the plate that remained empty, that sat in front of the seat he hadn't occupied since the day he had quietly packed his saddlebags, mounted his horse, and ridden away from our home in Bethel Creek.

Mother refused to believe that Papa had left her for good, shut her mind against the thought, and barred any of us from even mentioning his absence. We were to go on as if he still lived with us, still ate with us, still got up every morning to check on his properties and workers and investments.

So we went on with our charade, much to the astonishment of Bethel Creek, who caught on after some time that Papa was no longer present and that no explanation of his mysterious departure would be forthcoming.

My father became an invisible man who haunted our lives. If he had died, it would have been another matter. We would have buried him, mourned him. After time had passed, we would have slowly stopped talking about him or to him every day and simply lived the lives we had left.

Yet my mother refused to let him go, although he had already gone. To the townspeople, she became a grass widow, a woman whose husband hadn't even bothered to divorce her but had simply vanished and left her in much the same circumstances as a woman who had lost her husband through death.

For a long time, I didn't know what to do. My brothers gave Mother a wide berth at first, refusing even to speak with her as long as she insisted on speaking to Papa as if he were standing there in the flesh. Poor Jeremiah, three years old at the time, couldn't fathom what had happened to the man who gave him pony rides and twirled him in the air.

Papa was a man of strength and stability. We could set the old grandfather clock in the hall by his movements and habits. When he left, the household, like the clock, began running out of control, and it would take nearly a year before it became anything close to being regulated.

But it never kept good time again.

Mother kept up the charade, and we kept it up alongside, with no end in sight. I suppose it simply became a part of our everyday life, and we chose to go along in silence rather than opposition.

Charley and I soon finished taking care of the dishes, and I put Jeremiah to bed, while the others went about their own interests. Micah sat in the parlor reading Dickens while Theodore, Wilson, and Nehemiah pored over their scrapbooks. Each was fascinated with the burgeoning world of flight and were planning to build their own biplane, so they could swoop over the farm and frighten us all to death with their gravity-defying aerobatics. They frequently begged old newspapers from train travelers who disembarked in Bethel Creek for a respite. At home, they decimated the pages with scissors, cutting out every reference to aviation, military or civilian.

Charley and I sat in the corner, talking about war.

"President Wilson has no business sending you away," I said, taking up my sewing basket and continuing a piece of embroidery I had begun the evening before. It was a pillowcase embroidered with pink roses that I planned to place in my trousseau on the off chance the man of my dreams came walking through Bethel Creek one day. He certainly didn't live there at the time. I was convinced of that because I already knew about every potential mate who lived within a five-mile radius of town. Not that I was really all that anxious to be married, seeing as how I had spent all my waking hours looking after a houseful of men. I guess I hoped that I would have a family of girls to make up for the previous inequity of having only brothers who treated me the way I imagined Odessa and Pandora had been treated during slavery times, property at their beck and call.

"It's for a greater cause than selfish interests, Wren," Charley replied gently. I had begun to see him as more of a father figure since our real papa had left. He had overseen the farm and the sharecroppers who raised the crops, and he had provided some stability to our household since Mother always seemed to be going off to help someone else's family rather than paying attention to her own.

"Nationalism," I muttered, pricking my finger with the needle. "We have imperialism right here in America, when women can't vote or have a say in matters. Women are the ones who bear the sons who get sent to wars. We should have some say in who is sending them there. I've seen what happens with the mustard gas." I recalled a patient Mother and I had visited, a boy just back from the trenches in France. Huge sores and blisters covered his skin; he would probably bear the scars for life.

Charley smiled and leaned back as he lit his pipe. Mother liked the smell of the smoke—I guess it reminded her of Papa—so Charley only lit up when she was away to avoid feeding her delusion. "Nothing bad's going to happen to me, Wren. I'll be fulfilling my duty. Don't tell me you won't support me in our cause?"

"I don't have a problem supporting you," I said, bending to my work. "It's the cause I have trouble understanding." The stitches began to blur. "I'll miss you."

Charley placed a hand on my arm. "You'll be all right. She'll be all right."

"When? He's been gone for three years, and nothing's been all right since." I raised my head and looked into his deep brown eyes. It seemed sometimes that he and I had become the parents to this brood of dreamers.

"In time, Wren." He rose and rubbed his hands together. "Well, I'll be saying good night and adieu." The boys came to attention and gathered around him. "I don't want to have any letters from our sister telling me what a hard time you're giving her."

The boys looked at each other, and I could see the mischief in their smiles. "We'll be good and help as much as we can," said Theodore.

"We won't even miss you," echoed Wilson.

Charley frowned. "Sorry to hear that. I'll try not to miss you, either." He mussed Wilson's hair before turning back and kneeling in front of my chair.

"Don't worry, Wren. I'll be back before you know I'm gone." He kissed me on the forehead and held my hand for a moment before standing and herding the boys upstairs before him.

I sat in the now silent parlor and put away the embroidery, lest my tears stain the fine linen cloth.

In the morning, I woke to discover Charley had left early to catch his train. I had missed seeing him off and was disappointed that I hadn't gotten to truly say goodbye. As I prepared breakfast, I heard the surrey coming up the lane and looked out to see Mother pull up short beside the front door and sit staring into the distance for several moments before getting out.

She came in and sat at the table, running her palms across the wood grain and shaking her head. I poured her a cup of coffee, brewed strong and black the way she liked it, and placed it before her. She gulped it like spring-water—I wondered that it didn't scald her throat. It could have been whiskey, judging by the way she drank.

"What is it, Mother?" I wanted to sit down, but I had a stove top full of sizzling skillets to attend to. "How is Miss Picklemeyer?"

Mother set the cup down and pounded her palm against the tabletop. "Wren, in all my years I have never seen such as I saw this past night."

I glanced back and could see the exhaustion and confusion that etched her face. Her hair had come loose from its pins, and wisps floated around her head like dandelion seeds on a breeze.

"You know those stories about dragons, Wren, the ones in the books your father and I read to you as a child and as we now do to Jeremiah? The dragons that breathe fire and death?" Mother's formal way of talking had a way of becoming even more formal when she was about to tell a story.

"Yes," I said as I removed sausages from a skillet.

"I believe I saw a woman become a dragon this past evening."

"You're not making sense."

"Miss Picklemeyer. Her fever raged throughout the night. Then blood shot from her nostrils like fire from a dragon's mouth." Mother spoke in a whisper, as if she truly was telling a fairy tale. "Her skin, Wren, her skin turned purple as if she had formed a giant bruise that covered her entire body."

"Heavens," I said, laying the platters on the table. I couldn't remember hearing such things. "What happened?"

"Then she died. As suddenly as she fell ill yesterday, she died." Mother threw her hands up and then plopped them into her lap. "Nothing I gave her made any difference. Patent medicines, my own concoctions. Nothing. She simply spewed out her life and gave it up as I sat there in awe of whatever this pestilence was that struck her."

I had never seen Mother so flummoxed. She had always been confident in her diagnoses, because she had learned at the knee of the best—her father, Dr. Seymour McRae.

Oh, how Mother wanted to become a physician herself. She had begged, pleaded with her father to allow her to attend medical school. But Mim had put her foot down—as Mother was doing with me now, I supposed—and Mother had been forced to settle on becoming Grandfather's nurse.

She often told me how she had studied Grandfather's medical books, much to Mim's dissatisfaction. Mim had specific ideas for how a woman should lead her life, and this allowed for marrying a doctor, not becoming one. Nevertheless, Mother defied her to the extent that she could, learning all she could while she had the chance, until Grandfather's own death, just as Mother married my father, Mallon Birdsong.

He was not the man my grandmother would have chosen, but he was my mother's true love and a man who understood her ambitions and dreams. That is, until the day he suddenly left her without foundation or footing, with no one left who truly understood her. Except maybe me, and even I was often confused by her self-formulated beliefs and ideas.

I sat at the table, watching my mother close her eyes and pray silently, her lips moving, unable to discern the words she uttered to her unseen Lord.

27

Directly she opened her eyes again and focused on the plate I had set before her.

"Child, this sustenance is exactly what a woman needs after the sights I have just witnessed." She began eating as if she had worked days in the field. My brothers filed in and ate silently. I decided they were sad about Charley's departure—he was a father figure to them as well. I looked after Jeremiah, who viewed our mother with her wild hair and dazed expression with something akin to fright, but I reassured him she was only tired after having cared for a sick woman all night. She stopped eating for a moment and reached for her bag, pulling out a small package wrapped in brown paper and handing it to me.

"What is it?" I loved packages and always opened them slowly to maximize the pleasure gained from the surprise.

"I saw Charley off this morning," she said, wiping her mouth. "He left that for you. He said he had forgotten to give it to you last night."

Pulling off the wrap, I found a copy of *My Antonia*, a new novel by Willa Cather. Charley was especially sensitive to my interests and had probably noted my earlier admiration of Miss Cather's works.

"He said he had ordered it for your birthday, but since he wouldn't be here, he wanted to give it to you now."

My birthday wasn't until November, and Charley would likely be making his way to some European battlefield by then. I ran my hands across the cover and breathed in the aroma of the new leather binding.

"When do you suppose we'll see Charley again?"

"Sometime in this life or the next."

"Mother!" The callousness of the statement threw me off guard.

"We never know what lies in the course of a day, child. Last night was proof of that." She got up and carried her plate to the sink before going over to Jeremiah and leading him away to prepare him for school. "It is all up to the Lord and his infinite will."

I sat at the table and watched my brothers finish eating until they drifted away one by one. Left alone to consider the mysteries of God's will, I wondered why, if God is in charge of what happens, he could not make this war stop and prevent one innocent lady from becoming a human dragon. More questions that had no answers. They seemed to be the only kind I knew to ask.

2

WAITING FOR LIBERTY

I always wanted to meet someone mysterious and wise, someone who would tell me the reason for my life, my purpose in being. Someone like an angel. Of course, as Mother was fond of reminding me, the apostle Paul tells us that sometimes when we entertain strangers we may be entertaining angels in disguise. I wondered if this were true and, if so, where in the world was my angel hiding?

I pondered these ethereal thoughts while I washed the breakfast dishes. I did my best contemplation and had my most worthy thoughts and ideas when I was exposed to water—bathing, washing my hair, wading in the creek, even washing the dishes. In my mind that was the best use of dishwashing time, to consider the great philosophical, intellectual, and spiritual conundrums that perplex us. Of course, I had few high-minded revelations when doing the laundry. That was just plain drudgery. Some activities were antithetical to the production of epiphanies.

My muse was interrupted again after Mother saw Jeremiah off to school, when she ordered me to go over to Mim's and see to her possible needs.

"Why do I have to see to her?" I asked, whipping off my apron and tossing it onto a chair. "Odessa and Pandora are supposed to do that."

"They're more ancient than your grandmother," Mother replied, pulling out her hairpins and shaking out her long, thick hair. Where before it was a honey blond, it had mellowed with streaks of gray. I loved to brush those thick tresses in the evenings before bedtime, feeling its silken lengths and wishing my own dark brown hair was as lush and dusted with light. "Do not question me, child. I am too worn with confusion." She ran her hands through her fabulous tresses, her crown, and whisked away to her room for a nap, closing the door behind her.

I packed a basket with some baked sweet potatoes, the first of the season, along with biscuits, fresh-churned butter, and a jar of blackberry jelly. I then went to the barn, where I saddled and mounted my horse, Pegasus, and we made our way down the winding road to Mim's.

Mim lived in a small house now, just four rooms in one story. After Grandfather died, Mim decided she no longer wanted to take care of our large, rambling farmhouse and deeded it to Mother, which would have been Grandfather's wish anyway. Mother's brother, Frederick, lived in San Francisco. No one thought it likely he would ever return to Bethel Creek, having grown accustomed to city ways. Even after the Great Earthquake back in 1906, when his apartment building was destroyed, he chose to stay despite the risks of being overtaken by the Pacific

Ocean. He wrote that he knew worse places to be. Mother scoffed, saying that must include Bethel Creek, although she couldn't see why.

So Mim moved into a smaller house that had once belonged to the plantation's overseer during that legendary War of Northern Aggression. A plain wooden structure, it had two bedrooms—one for Mim, the other shared by Odessa and Pandora—a kitchen, and a spacious parlor. The three women could usually be found either sitting around the stove, rocking away the autumns and winters, or sitting on the porch, rocking away the springs and summers. As this was an unusually warm day, I found them rocking on the porch. Riding up the lane, I heard Odessa and Pandora singing:

> If 'ligion was a thing money could buy,
> I ain't gonna lay my 'ligion down,
> Well, de rich would live, en de po' would die;
> I ain't gonna lay my 'ligion down.
>
> But I'm so glad God fixed it so,
> I ain't gonna lay my 'ligion down,
> Dat de rich must die as well as de po';
> I ain't gonna lay my 'ligion down.

Odessa and Pandora had once belonged to my great-grandparents. I could never get used to saying that they had been "owned" by my ancestors. It was too difficult to think that these feisty women had once been someone's property, like a goat or a plow or a wagon. Once, while plundering a cedar chest in Mother's room, I ran across an old account ledger. Inside was a list of names with dollar amounts penned neatly alongside—the slaves and their valuations. It chilled my blood so that I slapped it shut and buried it at the bottom of the box.

Mim spotted me first and came down the steps to greet me. I got down from the horse, tied him to the porch railing, and ran to her.

"Wren! Oh, I was thinking of you when I woke up," she cried, wrapping me in an embrace. I could smell the lavender-scented soap she had used to wash her face that morning. Mim refused to use lye soap and ordered special scented soaps from fancy Paris mail-order companies. In French. She may have objected to my mother receiving higher education, but that hadn't stopped her from having a cultivated one herself.

"What were you thinking about me?" I leaned back and gazed into her eyes. They were azure in shade and made me think of the ocean, which Mother had seen when she and Papa took their honeymoon at the beach. Mother had often described the crashing waves and the foamy surf, the wind that blew from lands far away. I hoped that one day I would see it for myself. One of many things I hoped for.

"About how I wish it would work out for you and the Lowe boy to get married."

I pulled away and flounced onto the porch. Odessa and Pandora stopped singing, acknowledging my arrival with nods. They rarely spoke in my presence—or anyone else's for that matter—but when they did, it was usually something that nearly turned you on your head.

"Mim, you know that's not possible," I said, handing her the basket. She opened it, and the sisters tore into the sweet potatoes like ravenous birds. Mim went into the house and came back out with plates and utensils.

"I cannot understand why you will not even speak to him," Mim replied, taking a biscuit, splitting it neatly crosswise and filling it with jelly. "Sloan Lowe comes from one of the oldest, most reputable families in Rutledge County. I don't see how you could make a better match. Besides, he's guaranteed to live, having been excluded from the draft and all."

I studied the hydrangea bushes that ringed the house. They always bloomed blue, never pink, like they did when planted in certain soils. "There's something that isn't right about Skeeter," I said. "Something's missing in his mind."

"Oh, pish posh," she said, finishing off the biscuit. "And don't call him Skeeter. Nicknames are so common."

Everyone but the adults called Sloan "Skeeter." He had received the nickname not for his physical appearance, which was stocky and muscular, but for a high-pitched hum he produced when working up to one of his famous practical jokes or trying to throw the Sunday school teacher off her lesson.

I couldn't say that Skeeter Lowe had ever been what you'd call "sweet" on me because sweet was not a component of his personality. At times he had seemed more obsessed than anything else—following me around incessantly, sitting outside our house in his flivver waiting for me to come and go, hounding my friends for my every thought and move when we weren't together. Sometimes I went with him just to keep from having to explain myself.

It finally wore on me to the point where I nearly suffered a nervous exhaustion, as Mother diagnosed it. I couldn't sleep, couldn't eat, couldn't concentrate on anything anyone said to me. This disturbed Mother no end because she depended on my concentration more than anyone else's. She finally went to Skeeter's father and explained the situation. Later, we received word that he had beaten Skeeter within an inch of his life to make him leave me alone. Although I considered myself a pacifist, I couldn't say I felt sad to hear the news. It meant an end to being harassed. Finally, I could take a walk or sit in my own parlor without feeling that my every move was under scrutiny.

I couldn't convince Mim of Skeeter's baser nature, however. She only saw the family name and a chance to tie ours with theirs, to create a new Rutledge County dynasty, with myself as the new matriarch to bear forward the family standard.

"Mim, I will not marry a man who is crazy, and that's what Skeeter is, crazy, plain and simple." I closed the basket and started down the steps. I was stopped short by Odessa's voice.

"Watch out for that boy," she said, crumbs falling from the corners of her mouth. "The devil's brought him onto this earth for evil doin's."

Pandora nodded in agreement and began to sing:

Time, time, time is windin' up,
Time, time, time is windin' up,
Oh, destruction is dis lan', God's done moved His han'
En time is windin' up.

Mim stared them down, and they stopped singing, staring at me with pity like I was somehow cursed. "Don't pay them any attention, Wren," she said, coming down the steps and kissing my cheek. "They've been quite odd lately, singing about the end of time and all sorts of ill forebodings. Superstitions left over from slave days." She added this last in a whisper.

It seems some people have a better grasp on situations than others. I would take the freed slaves' opinions over Mim's any day.

I couldn't bring myself to go home just yet as I enjoyed the ride through the late summer sunlight. Pegasus seemed to enjoy himself as well, so we sauntered for a while down the deserted road. I decided it would be a good day to visit Miss Lanie.

Miss Lansdale's Academy for Young Ladies was on the outskirts of Bethel Creek. A dignified red brick structure, it stood straight and tall between massive live oaks as if to amplify Miss Lanie's admonitions regarding good posture. Riding up the oak-bordered allée, I could see she had turned the girls outside for fresh air and rigorous exercise, something else Miss Lanie advocated. Dressed in immaculate white outfits specifically designed for such outings by their benefactress, they were running about the tennis courts, spending more time ducking errant balls than actually playing the game. I spotted Miss Lanie sitting on the veranda, cooling herself with an elegant Japanese fan.

"Do as I say and not as I do again?" I said mischievously, taking a seat on the banister.

"Why, Wren, you know I must guard my sensitive skin against these harsh Southern sun rays," she replied, smiling and reaching for my hand, which she held and squeezed with sisterly affection. "I do so miss your smiling face in class these days. You were ever so much more motivated than these hellions I must now endure."

I blushed at Miss Lanie's assessment. I loved school dearly and wished that I could return here rather than spend my days looking after my brothers and filling in for my mother's increasing absences. "My time here was surely better spent than it is now."

"I take it your mother has not relented in her desire that you pursue your biblical duties to become a wife and mother rather than seeking more worldly satisfactions, although given the chance I am positive I could convince her that college is not at odds with scriptural precept."

Like my mother, Miss Lanie fancied herself a Bible scholar, having studied Greek, Hebrew, and even a smattering of Aramaic in hopes of someday producing her own interpretation of the Bible. Of course, she opposed Elizabeth Cady Stanton's *Woman's Bible* as heretical, but Miss Lanie was not averse to putting her own interpretations on the inspired Word of God.

"I don't know that it would do any good for you to speak to her," I said, examining a callus on my palm I had failed to notice before. It pained me that Miss Lanie may have felt it; she put such stock in women having porcelain skin and ravishing locks of hair. We wanted the vote, of course, and sometimes that meant expressing our views in public; however, we were quite certain that we wanted to look fetching when the men stopped to listen. Having the vote and having a husband and children, in our minds—and in the minds of most suffragettes—were not diametrically opposed premises.

"I was speaking in class today of Mrs. Boissevain," she said, a pensive look coming over her face. "What a brave woman she was, to have stood up for what she believed in and lived it, even unto the point of death."

Inez Milholland Boissevain was Miss Lanie's heroine for all time. Miss Lanie had no use for singers or actresses or even such esteemed characters as Florence Nightingale, although she taught us of her many virtues as part of a substantive education. The difference for Miss Lanie was that she had seen Inez Milholland Boissevain in the flesh and carried the memory like a torch against the black hours of night.

Before coming to Bethel Creek, Miss Lanie had enjoyed a privileged upbringing in the Northern states, with parents who were both politically aware and strongly connected with those in positions of power and influence, whether industrial, social, or political. In 1913, Miss Lanie had attended Woodrow Wilson's inauguration and was present at an electrifying moment in women's suffrage.

Eight thousand suffragettes, regaled in white, marched on Washington that glorious day, seeking legitimacy and attention for their cause. Leading the way, dressed in flowing robes, mounted on a white horse like a Greek goddess, was Inez Milholland Boissevain. An attorney, athlete, writer, and later even a war correspondent, she was a charismatic leader during a time when our cause badly needed someone to focus its energies.

At that moment, she became Miss Lanie's heroine, and Miss Lanie could not sing her praises enough. The day Mrs. Boissevain died in 1916, a victim of pernicious anemia, the result of having neglected her own health in favor of her beliefs, she became a martyr for suffragists everywhere. Miss Lanie had aspirations of taking up her mantle and leading a second charge on Washington.

Miss Lanie soon found that when she moved to South Carolina, however, she had not entered a region friendly to her cause. She endured a great deal of hostility and outright rudeness regarding her outspokenness. So she contented herself on influencing our thoughts away from those of our parents, albeit in a subtle fashion.

"I often wish that I could go to Washington and echo Mrs. Boissevain's final words to Mr. Wilson," she said, breaking my reverie. She stood and walked to the top of the steps where she caught the attention of the girls who were now quite worn with their poor attempts to master their game.

"It is time for all women to stand with their men at the polling places and cast our votes for the candidates we believe will lead all people forth to prosperity and health in this great democracy of ours," she exclaimed, spreading her slender arms as if to wrap them all in a giant embrace. "We have earned this right through our sweat and toil and belief and love and sacrifice for those we love and care for each day." She grabbed me and pulled me beside her. "In the profound final words of our esteemed martyr, the embodiment of our cause, Inez Milholland Boissevain . . ." At this she whispered to me, "Say it with me, Wren." I nodded.

"Mr. President, how long must women wait for liberty?" we shouted in unison, joined by the girls on the court, who threw their rackets into the air and began an impromptu dance, which Miss Lanie and I joined until everyone collapsed, out of breath, and the cook rang the lunch bell, dispersing everyone but us two, who were now too tired to move.

"So what are we going to do about getting women out to support our cause in Bethel Creek?" Miss Lanie asked, still breathless but offering her hand to help me up. I walked toward Pegasus, who had watched all this calmly as if women went around shouting and dancing in the school yards every day in our sleepy little corner of Rutledge County.

"I think we should take the soapbox approach."

She tapped her chin. "I like it, Wren. Are you prepared for the hecklers and ignoramuses who will affront your ideas and arguments?"

"Yes. I have six brothers. A few hecklers are nothing."

She laughed and held Pegasus while I pulled myself into the saddle. "Oh, Wren, I do so wish you could come here and help me teach."

"So do I, Miss Lanie. I would love nothing better," I said before riding away and wishing right now that I could be a woman riding a white horse who dared to challenge presidents.

Arriving home, I found Micah in the parlor studying the latest issue of *National Geographic* magazine. It always amazed me that the charms of far-off lands would so greatly fascinate someone who refused to leave the farm. Perhaps he was trying to work up his courage. I didn't ask.

Titania and Tiberius, our marmalade tabby cats, sat on either armrest like furry sentries, watching over his studies. The cats seemed to be a great comfort to Micah, who had little in common with our brothers, confined as he was to the farm.

Micah saw me, laid down his magazine, and began stroking the cats' lovingly groomed fur. "I didn't hear you come in, Wren," he said. I loved hearing Micah speak—his voice was low and melodic. I often closed my eyes when he read aloud to me, just to enjoy those musical tones. "Mother said to tell you she had to return to town."

"What's going on?" I removed my hat and went to the kitchen, followed by Micah and the two vocal felines. Some biscuits were left over from the night before, so I crumbled them in a bowl with milk, placing it on the floor. Titania nudged Tiberius from the bowl, asserting her dominance. *At least a cat can declare her proper place,* I thought.

"Three more people became ill, like Miss Picklemeyer," he said, taking a seat at the table, where he began peeling potatoes. He was the one brother I could count on to help with the household chores without being asked.

"That's peculiar," I replied, putting on my apron. "We're barely past summer, and it's not time for people to be getting ailments like the grippe."

Micah shrugged. "I don't know. She went to see about them anyway."

"Did she want me to come along later?"

"No, she said for you to stay here until she could get some idea about what's going on."

I watched Micah skillfully remove the potato skins, rinse the potatoes in a pan of water, then slice them into a pot. I poured fresh water over them and set them on the stove to boil. "You should have come with me to Mim's."

A shadow passed over his face; it was quickly replaced by a thin smile. "Were the sisters in their best form this morning, then?" Micah sometimes affected a British accent, which he picked up from a traveler who ran out of money and wound up working on the farm until he could earn enough to move on.

"It's not that far away. Just a couple of miles."

He stared down at Titania, who slunk around his ankles in satisfied bliss, her tummy full of biscuits. "I can't, Wren."

"Someday you're going to have to pass the gate."

"I will. Someday."

My precious Micah. How I wished he would join the world instead of experiencing its joys vicariously through the words and images composed by others.

Deep inside, I knew why he wouldn't leave. Like Mother, he, too, waited for Papa's return and wanted to make sure he didn't miss it by being away. It was as if he had decided that he was the one chosen to wait, to mark off the days and evenings on the farm with the ever present cats at his side. I guess we were all waiting in our own ways. Mother and Micah had developed their own ways of doing so; the rest of us hid our hope.

I decided to let it rest for now. "I'm going outside for a bit."

"I'll keep an eye on the potatoes," Micah said, returning to his magazine.

I walked onto the back porch and surveyed the acres of land that filled the length of my vision.

Our land was among the most fertile and productive in the county, and Mother had made sure everything ran smoothly since Papa's departure. The peach orchards, the cotton and corn fields, the turpentine operation—everything hummed along as if nothing had changed. I walked down the steps and wandered past the vegetable garden, which Mother had been readying for fall plantings of mustard and collard greens, and entered the gate of her greatest challenge.

I called it Mother's Garden of Eden.

She didn't know that, or I probably would have been subject to a lecture on blasphemy or some such, but I thought it appropriate because she was attempting to create one place on earth that was perfect, not subject to human frailties and failings, the cruelties of war, the sundry vagaries of life and its emotional blindsides.

Mother had a list of every plant mentioned in the Scripture; each one that could possibly be grown in our climate was present here. Although autumn approached, the changing seasons could not dim my own vision of the garden's fading beauty.

I leaned down and picked a sprig of mint to nibble as I wandered around the stone-paved lanes she had instructed the boys to assemble, insisting that such a garden was as much for contemplation as for sustenance.

The herbs were still fragrant although Mother had already harvested many of them. Rosemary, basil, chives, fennel, marjoram—they dried in bunches hung from the ceiling of the screened porch. Yellowing cucumber vines snaked across the rows of her vegetable section. I plucked a couple of ripe fruits from the ground, probably the last we would enjoy as few blossoms were left. Onions and garlic had been harvested and stored. Mother had crushed the coriander seed and added it to her apothecary, a remedy for dizziness when smelling salts were unavailable.

Just the day before, she had been digging, readying the plot for paper-whites and tulips. I wandered past the apple tree, which was filled with green knobs, and my mouth watered for apple pie, surely not a dish enjoyed in Bible times. I wondered if they cooked apples then, perhaps making applesauce or apple butter. Did a cookbook exist from the days of Jesus or Solomon? If one did, Mother surely would have known about it.

A grapevine curled through the arbor, a pitiful sight. Of all that was grown here, Mother agonized most over these sickly vines and pored over horticultural manuals, trying to figure out what she was doing wrong. If only she worried that much about her children.

I sat on a small wooden bench Mother had placed between the apple and willow trees. The garden's sorry state seemed to me much like our family—aged in spots, dying in others, sprouting new life in unexpected places. Although we all lived under one roof, it seemed that we had all sprung from different lands and at times didn't even speak the same language.

How I longed to be someplace else, someplace where I could learn and grow in my own way and pursue my interests uninterrupted. I wanted to shout my beliefs from the street corners and march through the placid avenues, wearing immaculate white regalia, stirring the masses to action.

Instead I cooked potatoes and washed clothes by the hundred pound, canned tomatoes and darned socks while my mother ran about healing the ills of the townspeople or poring over her precious herbal potions and medical and horticultural tomes. After Papa left, it seemed she had decided that mothering was no longer up to her and, as I was the lone female child in a family full of males, the mothering was now up to me.

She had no idea how much I resented my role, that I resented having it thrust upon me in a way that I hardly noticed. Oh, it had started out innocently enough. "Wren, would you please cook supper while I dash over to Mrs. McDuffie's to check on her ague?" "Of course, Mother."

Soon I was *of coursing* all the time, and it hadn't ended. What was worse, Mother now expected me to accompany her on her errands as well. She was grooming me to take over for her in all aspects, regardless of my own hopes and wishes.

At the age of seventeen—well, almost—I felt old and put upon. And she didn't even notice.

"I must speak with your father about getting us one of those automobiles."

I sprang from the bench, startled, knocking my head against a branch of the apple tree, loosening a ripe apple that fell onto my foot. Mother saw what happened and laughed. "I don't see what's so humorous," I said, rubbing my aching noggin.

"Wren, dear, after these past two days, I needed to laugh at something, and you merely provided the most convenient opportunity." She walked about the garden, leaning over here and there to snatch a weed from the dry ground. "I declare. Life is certainly a mystery to me. I suppose that's why I spend so much time in books, searching for the answers, although I daresay just discerning the clues is trouble enough."

As usual, her intellectual meanderings made no sense to me, so I plopped back down on the bench and just listened. Not that she would have given me a choice. Had I left, she would have followed me and continued her musings.

Mother stopped and leaned against the willow tree. "Three more people are ill with whatever afflicted Miss Picklemeyer. Honestly, I don't know what it is."

"I thought you said it was pneumonia."

"At first that's what I thought, but the symptoms don't correlate. This ailment acts more quickly. I don't know whether these others will live or not." She shook her head and knelt in the herb patch, running her palm over the unruly foliage. "My remedies are doing little for anyone."

"Perhaps they ate something bad," I said. "There was a supper over at the Presbyterian church the other night."

"I don't believe so. These symptoms differ from those of a food sickness." She motioned me to her side. "I must think about this. I'll look to you to prepare supper and supervise Jeremiah and Nehemiah's studies. Theodore and Wilson will arrive soon from the fields."

"I saw Miss Lanie today," I said, brightening, trying to distract myself from the chores at hand. "We're planning to speak on soapboxes, to encourage the townsfolk to support our cause."

Mother stopped and looked me in the eyes. Her direct gaze could have the effect of a hand pushing on one's chest, as if to drive you back into yourself.

"You know I disapprove of that woman's methods. You'll come to trouble if you insist on pursuing these outlandish ideas of hers. She's trying to use you for her own purposes." She stared at the surrey in the yard. It was still quite a serviceable vehicle, though the seat covers were worn through in places and the fringe missed a few teeth here and there. "I have no idea what an automobile costs. Do you suppose your father would know?"

I said nothing for several moments. My response when she began bringing up Papa was simply to plow ahead with whatever it was I had on *my* mind. That was her way, and it served her well. I found myself adopting it out of self-defense.

"I think I'll use Miss Jane Addams's arguments as part of my speech. She is quite persuasive. That is, until I come up with some unique thoughts of my own."

"How would I learn to drive?" Mother said, putting her arms out in front of her to pantomime a steering wheel. "I suppose Charley could teach me when he returns from his term of service. He often drove Reverend Berry's REO around town on errands."

Reverend Berry's REO Speedwagon was legendary for being the first motorized vehicle nearly everyone around here had seen in the flesh. He used it both for personal use and to help make deliveries for the general store. One day the engine backfired in the center of town, and you would have thought Gabriel had blown his horn for all the chaos it caused.

"It would make it so much easier to get around to everyone I need to see. Don't you agree, Wren? Of course, you could learn to drive it, too."

This piqued my interest. Miss Lanie had an automobile on order and was looking for the train to deliver it any day now. Perhaps she would teach me how to drive. Horses and Miss Lanie often didn't agree, although she was a proponent of excellent horsemanship as a matter of proper feminine breeding so as to mix with the upper social classes, should one be called upon to do so.

"I wonder if Mrs. Boissevain could drive?" I wondered aloud. "She could do most anything else, you know."

Mother and I had wandered along until we came to the back steps. When we went into the kitchen, the potatoes had boiled dry and smoke was roiling from the pot, blueing the air.

"Micah!" I screamed as Mother threw water on the pot before grabbing it with her apron and throwing it into the yard, where it smoldered in the dirt.

Bewildered, my brother ran into the kitchen. A quick glance at the stove revealed the story. "I was reading, and I'm afraid Titania's purring put me to sleep."

Mother watched the indifferent cat curl around his ankles and began laughing again.

"For the love of a cat the pot was lost," she said, and wandered away, leaving Micah and me to wonder if our mother would ever make sense to us—or to herself.

3

SHADOWS

The citizens of Rutledge County bustled through the streets as if they were the grand avenues of New York or the elegant boulevards of Paris instead of the dusty, unpaved paths of Bethel Creek. Of course, I had no personal experience with either place. Only through my and Micah's voracious travelogue readings had we made our vicarious journeys—in some cases the imagination must make do with what exists. Here, it was a few dusty streets, lined with what passed for an inclusive shopping and business district.

A bank, a couple of hardware stores, a millinery and dress shop, along with several churches—the First Baptist, the First Methodist, and the First Presbyterian—lined the main street. A livery stable still catered to those of us who lacked motorized transportation. Only a few residents could afford automobiles, but one enterprising resident had set up a filling station and garage to service the vehicles.

Mother and I rode in the surrey, with Nehemiah and Jeremiah in the back, while Theodore and Wilson rode ahead on their horses, Saturn and Neptune. Jake plodded along, as if hesitant to enter the teeming streets where he would meet others of his overworked ilk.

"Can I get some candy at the mercantile?" Nehemiah asked, setting off a round of "Please, oh please!" from Jeremiah, who bounced up and down on his seat as if it were a joggling board.

"May I get some candy," Mother said, smiling and steering Jake toward a hitching post. "I imagine you may if you would agree to share it with me—providing you do not eat it all before we get home." After she stopped the surrey and hitched Jake next to Saturn, she dug into her purse and brought out several pennies, which she distributed between the boys. "Look after your brother," she instructed Nehemiah. "I do not want to have to come looking for you both like I did last Saturday."

"Yes, Mother," Nehemiah said, snatching the pennies before she could get all the words out. I noticed that he took our baby brother by the hand and guided him across the street, something I had never seen him do before. Perhaps he was starting to grow up. At twelve, it was about time he started to show a little responsibility.

"How would you like a new hat?" Mother asked. I couldn't believe what I was hearing and eyed her suspiciously. Mother generally believed in buying new items of apparel for us when we needed them, not just for sport, as she seemed to want to do now.

"Will I be needing this new hat for some special occasion?"

"None that come to mind." She looked across the street at the milliner's window. "Although you may want a winsome look that day you rise up on your soapbox and address the sullied masses."

My mouth fell open. She had been listening, although I'm not sure when. Mother rarely indulged my whims or plans, so I refrained from making any remark that might make her reconsider this momentary generosity.

"Don't just stand there, daughter, come along," she said, whisking across the street, oblivious to the havoc she created by not looking both ways. I followed behind more carefully.

Apparently everyone had decided that now was the time for a new chapeau. The Bethel Creek ladies oohed and aahed over Mrs. Lapis Cochrane's accoutrements, all bedecked with novel trims, styled by sight from the latest ladies' magazines and catalogs. Mother began to browse, which for her meant trying on hats in rapid succession, practically hurling them back onto their stands and making a line for the next table. Ladies eager for new adornments occupied all the mirrors and dressing booths, so I sat on a small chair in the corner, noting that Mother seemed to have her own ideas about what would look good on my head, although I observed that everything she had me try on seemed more her style.

"Oh, Huldah, that is quite flattering." Mrs. Cochrane came over and gave the hat a slight adjustment, poking a hat pin into Mother's bun. "You certainly have your mother's flair."

At that, Mother snatched out the pin and hurled the hat across the room. "Lapis, I do not have my mother's flair for anything, have never had, and do not wish to have."

Chatter halted. Gossip ceased. Babble and jabber concluded. Everyone's eyes turned to Huldah Birdsong, and I sought to become invisible, turning my face aside where a gown-attired mannequin conveniently hid it. I had never heard her speak this way of her mother, so her outburst surprised me.

Mother smiled at everyone, a sweet smile, but one without eyes. "I apologize to you ladies. I have lost two more patients in the past week and have been deeply mystified by their sudden passings. Their loss must have affected me more than I realize." She turned to Mrs. Cochrane, who clutched her throat as if afraid Mother might come after it next. "Lapis, please ignore my remarks. You are correct that my mother does have quite a flair for fashion, but it is one that I am afraid I have never shared, preferring intellectual preoccupation with issues of a more devout nature."

With that, she turned and left the shop, leaving me to make my own unobtrusive exit when everyone's attention turned back to baser and more mundane exchanges, many of which, I'm sure, involved that strange outburst from Huldah McRae Birdsong.

Outside, I breathed deeply and saw that Wilson and Theodore had occupied themselves by pestering Mr. Hayes, the auto mechanic. Mother had disappeared from view, although our surrey stood at its post. Jake observed the passersby with an aloof expression. I decided that I would go over to the post office and pick up our mail.

My arms were loaded when I emerged from the tiny building, and I had trouble hanging on to all the packages. I should have taken one of the boys with me, I knew, but I thought I could handle it all myself. Odd paraphernalia was always arriving these days—packages of strange shapes and odd uses, usually something dealing with aviation for Teddy and Wilson. Occasionally a weather instrument would arrive, or some packet of seeds for Mother's Garden of Eden, most of which never bothered to grow no matter how much water and manure she added.

Heading toward the surrey, someone jostled me, and the packages slid from my arms. I turned to accost the jostler, when I saw an arm reach down and begin retrieving the parcels.

"You would never accept help, would you, Wren?"

Skeeter Lowe. I yanked the package from his hand and began picking up the rest myself.

"I don't expect, nor do I want, help from you, Skeeter."

"How do you expect me to stay away from one as stunning as you?" he asked, speaking in that poetic manner that had enticed my affections before I learned better. "It's been difficult these many months, keeping away when all I want is to feel my lips against those silken locks."

He folded his arms and watched while I gathered the packages more carefully and began walking briskly down the street. I was aware of his gaze on me and searched the crowd for signs of Mother. I had stopped wishing for Papa's return, but now I wished fervently he would come riding down the street, sweep me up, and ride us both into the country fields like he used to do when I was a child.

Skeeter followed so closely that I could almost feel his breath on the nape of my neck. Had I a free hand, I would have brushed it away like so much lint on fabric. I chose instead to walk more quickly, ignoring him, although I knew him to be right on my heels. Just then, I glanced across the street and spotted the one person who always seemed to be around when I never needed her.

Thracia Mills leaned against the red brick Bank of Bethel, eating a strand of licorice. Did you ever know a person who always seemed to be wherever you were, and you could never figure out how they seemed to know where you would be? Thracia was that sort of person for me. She was always standing in the shadows or lurking in a corner, watching with that expressionless face of hers.

Other people had noticed as well that Thracia always seemed to be shadowing me, as if she were some kind of self-appointed guardian. Some even suggested she might be an angel. I had my doubts. She didn't look like any depiction of angels I had ever seen, and I had seen plenty in books of art. Da Vinci, Botticelli, Rembrandt—the great masters had a completely different idea of what angels looked like, and none of them even faintly resembled Thracia Mills.

Her hair was so black that in a certain quality of light it had a sheen of indigo—the strands gleamed like bird feathers in sunlight. Her eyes, too, were a translucent blue of a hue unmatched by anything I'd ever witnessed in nature. Her skin, however, was a different source of speculation. Rumor had it that Thracia was of Indian blood, maybe even full-blooded, but no one knew for sure. Some said she was what was called a Brass Ankle, one of a mysterious group of people thought to be descended from Turks or even Moors.

No one knew where she came from, where she lived, or even how she derived a living, although she always seemed to have money to pay for her purchases. I don't know how we even came to know her name, unless it was from Odessa or Pandora, who knew everything that happened in Bethel Creek, good or bad, and would tell you only if they felt the inclination or you offered them something they were hungry for that particular day.

If the use of words and the mouth defines speaking, then Thracia was sadly deficient, because personally I had never heard nor seen her speak to anyone. Still, those crystalline eyes spoke a language of their own, and right now they were focused directly behind me, on the face of Skeeter Lowe, and in a strange way, I felt grateful, for presently I realized that footsteps no longer dogged me. I had arrived at the surrey and, looking back, saw Skeeter retreating to the other end of the street, Thracia paralleling his steps from the opposite side, as if by watching him she were propelling him with her gaze somehow to leave me alone. I would have to tell Teddy and Wilson about it later. Perhaps they could find some way to harness Thracia's stare power to propel their aircraft off the ground.

Mother was sitting in the surrey, having made her purchases at the general store, and she was looking around, trying to see if Jeremiah and Nehemiah had heeded her warnings. "I saw Sloan following you," she said, continuing to scan the crowd.

"Thracia cast her evil eye on him," I said, laying the packages on the backseat and handing Mother the bundle of letters. "She's frightening, and I don't know whose following me around scares me worse, hers or Sloan's."

"Perhaps Thracia feels she has some sort of calling to be your protector," Mother said, taking the letters and stuffing them in her purse. Mother had a rule that I was not supposed to look at the letters until she had a chance to go through them first. She may have thought that if I saw something from Papa, I would take it away, hide it from her, prevent her from seeing it in some way, although I couldn't divine her reasoning for this. Of course, I could have cheated and looked, and she would never have been the wiser. However, her edict was strong, and I was too fearful to risk detection.

"I'm an adult now," I replied, sitting beside her. "I don't need a protector. Once I have the vote, I'll be as strong as any man and will state my case to anyone who hounds me."

Mother regarded me for a moment before she burst into laughter, which drew the attention of a group of men standing on the corner smoking cigars, probably discussing politics, a subject at which I felt I clearly excelled. At that moment I would have preferred their company to hers, although they were probably of the ilk that was denying me the right to my constitutional privileges.

"Daughter, I can always count on you to lighten the load of a day," she said, motioning to my baby brothers, whom she had spotted coming out of the livery. "Come on, boys," she called. "We must get your sister home before she begins locking up vagrants and handcuffing scofflaws to the village pillory."

I blushed and bowed my head, but I could hear the men laughing, whether at me or each other's jokes, I didn't know and now didn't care to find out. The boys jumped in the surrey and we pulled away, with Huldah Birdsong's laughter wending its way through the horses and dust and crowds of country people come to town on Saturday.

Our escape was short-lived. A man shouted behind us. "Mrs. Birdsong, wait!"

Mother pulled the reins and Jake lumbered to a halt. Leaning out, I looked back and saw it was Mr. Parsons, running and waving his hat in the air.

"A boy collapsed in the middle of the street, Mrs. Birdsong," he said once he stopped and caught his wind.

"How old a boy?" she asked, hesitating to turn the surrey around. She had been out two nights already this week, and I could see the bags growing beneath her eyes.

"About eighteen or nineteen. Fell hard and fast away."

"Did anyone remove him to some place more comfortable?"

"He's been taken to the livery and placed in a stall."

"You don't know who it is?"

"No, ma'am. He is a stranger in town. Maybe an enlistee on his way to the army camp. Probably got off the train."

Mother sighed and began pulling the reins so Jake would make the turn. "Wren, when we get there, I want you to take the surrey and drive Nehemiah and Jeremiah home."

"Mother, why can't they ride home with Teddy and Wilson? You may need my help." Although degradations had defined the day, I didn't feel ready to go home yet. I fervently wished Micah were here. We used to have so much fun. Instead he was home, probably reading Shakespeare's sonnets to two indifferent and uncomprehending felines.

"Yes, Mama, why can't we ride on the horses?" Jeremiah sucked a gumdrop, handing one from his crumpled brown paper sack to Mother over her shoulder. She looked back at him and smiled, taking the candy and popping it into her cheek. Ignoring Mr. Parsons, who looked now as if he desperately needed a ride back, she drove on ahead before giving her answer to my baby brother.

"Maybe, just this once, boys." She ran a palm across her forehead. "I don't know what's going on, Wren," she said to me quietly. "I've never seen such as this illness that is striking people."

I thought back to Miss Picklemeyer. "Are all their symptoms similar?"

"Similar, yet different." She stared ahead at the crowd that had gathered around the livery door. "I know now that it is not pneumonia, nor is it like any case of the grippe I have ever seen or heard my dear father describe. People turning all shades of blue and purple, like they've been bruised all over in a fight. Spitting up bloody mucous by the quart, by the gallon." She pulled Jake to a halt and got out of the surrey. Spotting Teddy and Wilson, she instructed them to take our brothers home, then motioned to me to follow her.

Inside the livery, some men had laid out the young man on a clean bed of straw and covered him with a saddle blanket. His breathing was raspy. Mother leaned down and listened to his chest.

"It's a death rattle," I heard a woman whisper.

"Would everyone please leave," Mother said, rising and addressing the crowd. She spread her arms and walked toward the group, which fell back as from an approaching squall. Perhaps word had already circulated about the outburst in the hat shop and no one wanted to induce another fit of pique. The crowd did as told, and soon it was only Mother, Mr. Parsons, the livery manager, and me.

Digging through her black bag, Mother brought out a vial and, with a medicine dropper, forced some liquid into the boy's mouth. He otherwise appeared to be in good health, muscular in fact, not the type one would associate with sudden fainting spells. She ran smelling salts under his nose, but this failed to revive him.

"The undertaker has already been right busy this week, Mrs. Birdsong," said Mr. Parsons, hunkering down and examining the contents of the boy's pockets.

"Are you taking up thievery now?" Mother asked, pulling out a stethoscope and listening to the boy's chest.

"I'm only trying to see who he is and where he's from, in case we need to notify next of kin."

"You have such little faith in my abilities?" I could see Mother's hackles rise like those of a mama cat confronting a threat to her vulnerable litter. It plainly vexed her that she was confronted with an ailment that defied treatment, resulting in the unexplained deaths of three people so far, now threatening the imminent death of another.

"Help me load him in the surrey," Mother said, putting his arm around her shoulders and lifting his torso.

"Mrs. Birdsong, you can't be serious!" Mr. Parsons stood with his hands on his hips. "You have no idea if this boy's a saint or a sinner."

"Why, Mr. Parsons, haven't you heard?" she said, as I came to her aid and we pulled the boy to his feet and dragged him across the dry floor. "We have all sinned and come short of the glory of God. Even if this boy is one of the least of these, at least we will have fulfilled our mission to the heavenly Father."

"I fear you're putting your family in grave danger. What if he's faking and once he arrives at your home, he wakes and murders you and your brood?"

Mother and I had managed to lay the boy across the backseat. I sat beside him to prop him up. Then Mother went over to Mr. Parsons, pulled him over to the surrey, and slapped his hand across the boy's febrile cheek. "Sir, you cannot fake that," she said as he snatched his hand away in disgust. "Now give me what you took out of his pockets."

Appearing chastened, Mr. Parsons reached into his jacket and gave Mother the boy's induction papers. "Jason Spurley," she read before folding it, placing it in her medicine bag, and taking the reins again. "Well, Jason, at least you won't have to spend the night with a bunch of mules."

At home, Mother busied herself in Charley's bedroom, turning it into Jason Spurley's sickroom. "I intend to discover what this ailment might be," she said to no one in particular.

Mother refused to let anyone sleep in the barn, even if we had a sick animal. She claimed that animals could transmit diseases to humans through prolonged contact and usually made me change my clothes after riding Pegasus.

I followed Mother's directions, trying to make this boy as comfortable as possible, meanwhile ruminating on my own objections to his presence here. Certainly, Mother and I had both seen the results of our share of contagious illnesses, and seeing that we might be on the verge of an epidemic was not difficult. But nothing stopped Huldah Birdsong when patients were in need.

I watched Jason's face. He had not regained consciousness on the bumpy road home and showed no sign of doing it now. His breathing was labored, his skin almost scalding to the touch. We sponged his body with cool water that Nehemiah brought from a flowing well down the road, water that many thought possessed curative powers. Many drank it as a safeguard against illness, taking it home in milk cans or simply stopping by daily for a long swig from a metal dipper someone had thought to hang from a nail driven into an old oak tree.

Mother had tried to force some of it down his throat, but he coughed it back out. She now sat in a chair next to the bed and stared at his face.

"Child, I do not know you, I only know that you are some mother's son," she said in a quiet voice, stroking his hand. "Wren, will you see to supper? I must stay here."

"I can stay with him," I offered, hoping maybe she would go downstairs and deal with the boys for once.

"No, child. I don't know but that his condition will take a turn for the better or more ill. I have already seen this. I do not wish you to witness his passing, if such is to occur."

I turned away. *I've seen people die before, Mother,* I thought, closing the door behind me. *Why is this different?*

I went downstairs and found Mim, Odessa, and Pandora perched on the parlor sofa like a three-headed Medusa. Titania and Tiberius sat on their haunches like Egyptian statuettes, staring at the three women. Odessa and Pandora had shut their eyes to avoid the cats' intensive stares. They had some idea that a cat could steal your soul with its eyes. I wanted to laugh at the scene, even more when I looked at Micah and noticed that his lips were twitching at the corners.

Mim perched on the edge of the sofa. "Wren, I hear your mother has foolishly brought home some stranger."

"Yes, she has," I replied, taking a seat in the velvet-upholstered gooseneck rocker. "You know she can't turn away anyone in need."

"That is not wise on all occasions," she said.

Eyes shut tightly, with Odessa beginning and Pandora following, the sisters began to sing:

> Jes' low down de chariot right easy,
> Right easy, right easy,
> Jes' low down de chariot right easy
> An' bring God's servant home.
>
> Jes' tip around my room right easy,
> Right easy, right easy,
> Jes' tip around my room right easy
> An' bring God's servant home.
>
> Jes' move my pillow 'round right easy,
> Right easy, right easy,
> Jes' move my pillow 'round right easy
> An' bring God's servant home.

They stopped, and I turned to see Mother standing in the doorway, her eyes blasting a hole through Mim's forehead.

"What are you doing bringing those heathens into my home, among my children?" Odd how Mother didn't mind sending me into their midst unprotected, but she objected to having her sons exposed to their jumble of ideas. How the sisters knew to stop singing, I didn't know, because both were still guarding their souls against cat gazes by keeping their eyes closed.

"They are not heathens, daughter; they are singing Christian Negro spirituals here," Mim said, rising from the sofa as if from a pew.

"They may be singing words borne of God, but they do not possess hearts given to the Savior," Mother replied. "They are captives of superstition and enchantments, and I want you all out of my house."

Micah and I exchanged glances. Although he didn't know about the outburst at the millinery, I felt sure he thought this all as odd as I did. Mother and Mim had never really gotten along—Mother was more her father's child, as I've explained—but they had never before been openly hostile. Now I was seeing an expression on Mim's face I had never seen before when she was confronted with Mother's anger. It was an anger of her own.

"I came to see to you-all's well-being," she said, promptly shooing away the cats, who ran up the stairs, where they continued their observations surreptitiously through the railings. "You can open your eyes now. The cats are gone."

Odessa and Pandora opened their eyes and stared at Mother, who glared back. "Has everyone fallen deaf? I want you all out of my house."

"Miss Huldah, we brung you some bags of asafetida, thinkin' you might want to pertect your chilluns from what's ailin' that boy," Pandora said, offering a small sack to Mother, who took it and watched the sisters exit through the front door to their waiting carriage.

"You see, they don't bear any ill toward you," Mim said in a quiet voice, patting Mother's shoulder. I could see it was an effort for Mother not to shrug her hand away. "You might want to show a little more Christian charity toward them. They did help to raise you, remember?"

Mim smiled thinly before kissing me and Micah, then sweeping through the door, taking care to slam it loudly behind her.

I looked at Mother as she dug into the bag, bringing out the smelly remedy for all that ails you and muttering something under her breath. I leaned closer, but I couldn't catch her words. "What did you say?" I asked, taking the bag she offered and pulling the string over my head.

"Judge not lest ye be judged," she said, handing the bag to my brother and going out the back door, where she walked around the garden for hours, thrashing her arms and shaking her fist at the heavens, leaving me with five hungry boys and one sick stranger, whose illness was only a harbinger of events no one could have imagined.

4

SUFFRAGE

Jason Spurley lived through the night.

It was a small victory for Mother, who had already grown weary of having her patients drop dead so early in their infirmities. She now lay sleeping in her own room, her nose tucked against Papa's pillow, which she had refused to let me wash in all these years. I knew it could no longer hold his scent. Once I expressed my dismay at her lack of hygiene, much to my detriment. Her tirade and the look of betrayal on her face were more than I could take. I wound up fleeing to the hayloft, where I stayed with the barn kittens who mewed softly at my own distress.

Papa's leaving had been hard on everyone, and Mother tended to forget that the rest of us lost someone, too, that awful day. Furthermore, none of us knew why he was gone. We figured she knew, but in her grief, she wasn't going to tell. Perhaps that was why she left us alone more and more, putting not only distance between our bodies but distance between our hearts.

Watching her sleep, I felt some modicum of sympathy, an emotion I could rarely summon in her case. I had never known true love myself and had discovered that I was jealous of the feelings she and Papa had shared before. I wondered if I would ever have those feelings—or if someone would ever have those feelings for me.

But I had to put it all aside. Someone had to keep our household running.

As I went about my daughterly and motherly and wifely duties the next morning, those being the spectrum of my responsibilities, I began to formulate my soapbox speech, one that would dazzle the citizens of Bethel Creek with its intelligence and brilliance of phrase, its elegance and graceful delivery, as elocution was another strong aspect of Miss Lanie Lansdale's curriculum.

I had read the speeches of all the great female orators and writers of my time and the times before: Jane Addams, Elizabeth Cady Stanton, Susan B. Anthony, Sojourner Truth, Mary Wollestonecraft, and, of course, Mrs. Boissevain. In addition, I had read all the opposing viewpoints to our cause of women's right to vote and was prepared for all arguments.

Then there was my dress.

Made of pure white voile, it was a sight to behold. I had worked on it under lamplight, straining my eyes at the stitching, to Mother's chagrin. But being taken seriously was important. I should look as if I commanded attention. In this dress, I surely would, although I regretted that I hadn't gotten to pick out a proper hat to accompany my ensemble.

"Citizens of Bethel Creek," I intoned as I gathered laundry. "Our country stands on the precipice of great change, one in which all citizens have the right and duty to participate."

Words churned in my mind. I wanted the right to vote, to have a say in the future and destiny of my beloved country, the great state of South Carolina, and the civic affairs of the humble little town of Bethel Creek. If women received the vote, why, perhaps I could run for public office!

The thought astounded me. It had never occurred to me that gaining the right to vote might also mean gaining the right to be voted for! I envisioned the headline:

WREN BIRDSONG ELECTED MAYOR
OF BETHEL CREEK

It was too much to anticipate. I mentally revised it:

WREN BIRDSONG ELECTED FIRST FEMALE
MAYOR OF BETHEL CREEK

I let my imagination fly. I could go beyond that—get elected to the state house, the state senate. Maybe even the White House!

Then a groan pummeled down the stairs and wrecked my reverie like a bull browsing a dining table set with china for twelve.

So much for dreams. Mother was asleep, and we had an ill stranger upstairs.

I went to Jason Spurley's bedside. Mother had piled the bed with so many quilts, I could hardly find him. He was still feverish, but not as much as before. Apparently, some of Mother's medicines had finally worked. I poured cool water over a cloth and placed it on the young man's forehead. He opened his eyes, and a wan smile passed over his face.

"Did I die?" he asked, reaching for my hand. I backed away.

"No, sir, you are still very much alive and occupying a room meant for a well person."

I hadn't known I felt that way until the words slipped out and slithered across the room.

"Then may I know your name, since I am quite convinced that you are no angel."

I folded my arms. "My name is Wren Birdsong. You are here because my mother, Mrs. Huldah Birdsong, took pity on you and brought you to our home, where you are to recuperate from your illness."

"For that I am exceedingly grateful, *Miss* Birdsong." He closed his eyes. I stepped closer to the bed. He opened one eye, and I stepped back. "Are we connected with invisible strings?" he asked. "Every time I look at you, you withdraw. Has my illness caused me to hallucinate?"

Blood rushed to my face, and I turned toward the window, which I opened for some fresh air. Mother was a firm believer in fresh air for the sick. Though a cruel west wind had begun to blow the first hint of autumn chill, I thought the atmosphere might do Mr. Spurley good.

He pulled the covers around his neck. "And just where would your mother be about now?"

"She's exhausted from looking after you, but she's right downstairs, within shouting range."

"Good to know," he said. "I'm not sure I trust you. Could I trouble you for some water?"

I hadn't noticed until then how weak his voice was, or how hoarse. I started out the door and ran into Mother, who was tucking pins into her hair. She smiled warmly at Jason.

"I thought I heard voices, and it wasn't time for the boys to come in yet." She went to our patient, felt his forehead and cheeks, and peered into his eyes. She seemed exultant over her triumph. "Son, you are much improved. Wren, hurry downstairs and fix Mr. Spurley some broth."

"Beef or chicken?" I asked. "Or vegetable. Perhaps I can round up some radishes that might suit Mr. Spurley's appetite."

Mother glanced over her shoulder at me. She had been feeling Jason's extremities for swelling and the top of his head, perhaps for the nubs of horns. "Whatever you've got, daughter. I'm sure most anything would be fine for our patient. Isn't that right?" She turned and smiled into his eyes.

"Mrs. Birdsong. Miss Birdsong," he added, looking at me with what I perceived to be a wink, although I'm not sure, he was so hoody-eyed with sleep. "I would be honored to have anything either of you concocted to come across these parched and weary lips."

I went down the stairs. "Parched, maybe," I muttered. "Weary, my foot."

Titania and Tiberius followed Micah first through the kitchen, where he retrieved a tea cake, and then into the parlor, where he proceeded to read *Hamlet* aloud, as if felines would care whether Hamlet really wanted to be or not to be. Since they all seemed oblivious to me, I went back to my speech preparations.

"Citizens of Bethel Creek, women have earned . . ."

Somehow the word *earned* didn't sound right.

"As with our forefathers, women possess the inalienable right to vote."

I explored our well-stocked pantry until I found a Mason jar of beef broth, which I opened and poured into a pot on the stove. Micah had launched into Hamlet's soliloquy:

To be, or not to be: that is the question:
Whether 'tis nobler in the mind to suffer
The slings and arrows of outrageous fortune
Or to take arms against a sea of troubles,
And by opposing end them?

"We have been the victims of the outrageous fortunes of times and men," I improvised, thinking William Shakespeare would have made an excellent ally in the suffrage movement. I also recalled a story Miss Lanie had told us about how the North Carolina legislature, when presented with an act to legalize women's right to vote, in turn referred the legislation to the Committee on Insane Asylums.

Mother came downstairs and peered into the pot. "What is all this talking down here? Mr. Spurley needs his rest."

"Mr. Spurley is not as infirm as you would believe," I replied, exasperated that I was never going to get my speech in one piece before Saturday. We had already violated all the Sabbath traditions and were going about business as if it were an ordinary day. "He was quite fresh with me earlier. Said he couldn't trust me. Can you imagine that? Here we are taking him into our home, into the bed of my brother who has gone away to serve in some unholy war, and he has the gall to say he cannot trust me."

Mother was preoccupied. She stared out at her garden. "I see that if we are to wage war against this infection that is sweeping our town, I shall have to put on the full armor of God along with a large kettle and replenish my apothecary." She went to a drawer in the dining room and pulled out her cookbook of brews, rightly titled *General Directions for Collecting and Drying Medicinal Substances of the Vegetable Kingdom: List and Description of Indigenous Plants, etc.; Their Medicinal Properties, Forms of Administration, and Doses*, published in 1862 by the Surgeon General of the

Confederate States of America. Mother wasn't one to relive the Late Unpleasantness, but she frequently called this manual one of the best ideas to come out of the late, great Confederacy.

She thrust a basket at me and motioned for me to follow her outside.

"What about Mr. Spurley's broth?"

"He fell asleep before I left the room," she said, pinning a wide-brimmed hat on her head. The day was fair and sunny, and Mother despaired of developing a freckle, much the same as Mim. I grabbed a basket from the porch and followed, reprieved from having to face our patient again. We went behind the barn, where Mother had set up a small shed exclusively for drying herbs and other plants she deemed necessary for her healing arts. It seemed Mother had an elixir or potion or salve for just about anything.

"We do not know exactly what this illness is, Wren, so we are going to approach it symptomatically," she said, taking down jars from a shelf she had made Charley build before he left for the war. "We shall create remedies for coughs, nostrums for fevers, relief for chills, panaceas for aches, and whatever else we can think of to help these unfortunate victims."

"I wouldn't call Mr. Spurley unfortunate," I said under my breath.

"What, child? I didn't understand you." She surveyed the dried flowers and herbs that hung from the rafters, choosing stalks at random and laying them on a makeshift table, an old door laid across two sawhorses.

"I'm afraid Mr. Spurley is taking advantage of our hospitality," I replied. "I believe that if you examine him more closely you will see he is more a malingerer than a victim of any illness. I fear that we are his unfortunate dupes."

Mother snatched me around by my elbow, startling me into dropping the jars onto the hard-packed dirt floor. "Wren Birdsong, I will not have you going around calling my patients liars."

I looked into her eyes and set myself solidly on the ground. "You're too trusting, Mother. Mr. Spurley is quite well, well enough to make fresh remarks to me. He's far from death's door."

"You did not see the look in his eyes that I saw in the others," she said, letting go of my arm but keeping her eyes locked on to mine. "Child, your experience with mortal illness is sorely limited, and I would advise you to keep close counsel on such feelings that you have here expressed."

I had seen my share of the dead and dying, courtesy of Mother's attempts to make me follow in her well-worn footsteps. I knew what death and dying looked like. I also knew what a faker looked like, and Jason Spurley was one and the same.

We went silently about our work then, grinding and cutting and adding water to various mixtures of flora that she carefully mixed and measured. Odd scents pervaded the space, and at times I felt almost dizzy.

In some cases, Mother ground roots down to powder and tore apart leaves, placing them in packets that she could leave with patients. Teas were a common remedy in her arsenal. Of course, she also carried many patent medicines. Blood pills, liver pills, worm syrups, liniments, skin ointments, carbonic salve, camphorated oil, and an assortment of lozenges filled her black bag. Aspirin had become a reliable fever reducer, although she explained that some patients were now refusing it because it had come from Germany. We were at war with them, and a rumor was circulating that the Germans had imported this deadly bug in the tablets. Mother dismissed the rumor as war propaganda.

Mother worked in a frenzy close to obsession. I surmised she might be giddy with lack of sleep, which can cause odd behavior. Since Papa's leaving, she seldom slept through the night. I would frequently awaken to hear her pacing back and forth in the hall or climbing up and down the stairs, praying in a loud whisper, although not loud enough for me to discern the exact words. These prayers and pacings sometimes went on for hours, during which I failed to achieve my own goal of a sleep filled with dreams of converting the uneducated masses to my cause of women's suffrage and obtaining the ideal mate for life.

"Should I go and take Mr. Spurley some broth now?" I asked cautiously when I noticed Mother's efforts beginning to wind down.

She rubbed the back of her hand across her forehead. "Yes, child, I think that would be a good thing."

I turned around to find Jeremiah standing in the doorway.

"The man upstairs has stopped talking," he said.

"Perhaps he's asleep," Mother said, taking Jeremiah by the hand and leading him back toward the house. "Did you bother him? Did you wake him?"

"I just stood in the doorway. There's something red all over the covers."

Mother turned pale, let go of his hand, and ran straight into the house and up the stairs. I came right behind, pausing only to pull the pot of steaming broth from the hot eye. We had already lost one pot to carelessness and nearly set the house on fire then.

Upstairs, I found Mother sitting in the chair next to the bed, staring at the blood that seeped across the quilts and pillow, blood that had already begun to turn black from exposure to the air. Jason's mouth was open, his eyes stared at the ceiling, at nothing, at everything. I hesitated to think that he might be staring at eternity after all I had said about him.

Jason Spurley died at the end of the day.

Something dangerous happened to Mother after that. She became more lost to us than ever.

After the undertaker removed Jason, assuring Mother that he would take care of notifying the boy's family, Mother took to her bed and left everything, meaning the running of our household and the attempted control of my brothers, to me. I tried and tried to pry her out, especially when folks began sending for her to attend to the growing numbers of our neighbors who were becoming ill each day. Mother had done this before—withdrawn when she was faced with something she couldn't command into submission. Mim came by, with Odessa and Pandora in tow as always, and advised me to keep my distance from the townspeople, as an epidemic was afoot. I informed her that her warning was too late; we had already been exposed.

"It is beyond your mother's control," Mim said, coming out of Mother's room after a vain attempt to draw her out. "Either the hand of God is at work seeking redemption from his people, or it's the footwork of Satan seeking destruction among the righteous."

"Could it be that people are simply getting sick because they don't keep proper hygiene?" I asked. I had taken to scrubbing everything to a slick shine, and my hands were raw from all the hot water and abrasive lye soap. I rifled Mother's bag for purification potions, which I advised my brothers to take, much to their chagrin. Teddy and Wilson outright refused, so I bid them stay out of town, which they also refused to do. I could exert a little more influence over Nehemiah and Jeremiah, and dear, dear Micah would do anything I asked, save leave the property to get supplies when we ran dangerously low.

I decided I would kill the proverbial two birds with one stone. That Saturday, I would make the foray into town, make my soapbox speech, get the supplies we needed, and show Mother and Mim there was nothing to fear, that all this sickness was some sort of aberration, and that since we had already been exposed to Jason Spurley, we were thus immune and could continue with our business and lives as normal. Perhaps showing Mother that I could leave the house and live would be the thing that would draw her from her melancholy, which I knew to be more than just losing those few patients; it was the prolonged absence of Papa, who was her heart and soul and whom she couldn't really see, except in her mind, and only then as someone he used to be. I wanted her to know that our father had already abandoned us, his absence grieved us, and we didn't need to be abandoned by her presence.

Early Saturday morning I rose and donned my beautiful white dress. When I came downstairs, Micah was sitting at the table, peeling an apple, which he ate from the knife blade, much like Papa would do. He was also sitting in Papa's chair, which surprised me. It also gave me a little hope—maybe this sudden bold act meant he was working his way up to other changes.

"Mother will tan you within an inch of your life if she finds you sitting there," I said, snitching a slice of apple from him.

"I'll explain that I was tired of seeing the empty chair," he replied, his mouth full.

"She doesn't see it as empty. She sees Papa."

"She needs to stop."

"We all need to stop some things." I watched his expression, but it didn't change.

"Well, I guess this is one of those things."

I watched him for a moment, then decided the argument wasn't worth it. I needed his help, but I had other things planned for today. His being there wouldn't make a difference either way. "I'm going into town," I said. "I'm going to make a speech."

"Trying to convert the masses?" Micah asked, paring the apple down to the core.

"After a fashion," I replied, allowing myself a slight smile. I turned to pull on my wrap when Teddy, Wilson, Jeremiah, and Nehemiah filed into the kitchen. They looked at the cold stove in unison, then at the empty table, then at me.

"Where's breakfast?" Teddy sat down, and the others followed suit.

"You'll have to get your own." I proceeded to pull on my wrap and grabbed my purse, counting the money I had taken from Mother's cedar jewel box just moments before. She had lain in the bed, watching me through glassy eyes. We hadn't spoken. I just took the money and left her there to wallow in the dingy sheets and the perpetual dark produced by the drawn shades.

"Mother isn't well. It's your responsibility to feed us." Wilson held a rolled piece of paper in his fist—probably ill-conceived plans for another flying contraption. I had dreadful visions about finding them all dead one day, lying in a heap on the ground, crushed under the weight of some homemade craft that wouldn't dream of flying, even in the tailwinds of a hurricane.

"It's time you started feeding yourselves."

"But that's not what men are supposed to do," Nehemiah replied. "You're a woman now. I heard Mother tell you. So that's what you're supposed to do."

I held my breath for a minute so my blood would come to a full rolling boil. "I'm not *supposed* to do anything. If that means letting you helpless men get by on a sliced apple or cold biscuits, then so be it. I am your sister—not your wife, not your mother. I have a right to a life of my own."

"Women don't have lives of their own," Teddy said. "Y'all are put here to serve us. It goes all the way back to Eve. Mother'll tell you that."

"It may go back to Eve, but it's stopping with Wren Birdsong." I looked to Micah, who shrugged his shoulders. So much for favorite brothers. It turned out I couldn't count on any of them.

I glowered at Teddy. "I hope you can find a cliff to fling yourself off of with one of those airplanes. It would serve you right if it crashed in the valley and your bones were picked apart by vultures."

"Buzzards." Micah grinned.

"What?"

"We don't have vultures around here. He'd get picked apart by buzzards. There aren't any cliffs around here, either."

"Then jump off the bluff into the creek. I don't care. Just jump off something."

With that I took my leave. I hitched Jake to the surrey and made him trot as fast as his stubborn legs would go, until he began to huff. Suddenly I felt merciful toward the poor animal and pulled up, letting him rest for a moment before resuming our trek at a more reasoned pace.

I loved my brothers—truly I did. I loved them more than my own life. But what I disliked was feeling that my life was inextricably tied to theirs, that I was somehow responsible for taking care of every one of their daily needs. I even had the disturbing thought that this could go on even after they were married, or that if I married, I could not leave them all, Mother included, because it seemed I was so necessary to keeping the household together, to keeping everyone fed and clothed and sane and alive, as if they themselves did not possess the knowledge, nor could they get it, to do these simple activities for themselves.

Putting it out of my head, I concentrated on the road ahead. "My life is my own," I said to myself aloud, and Jake pricked up his ears. "I am a suffragette, and I will someday become mayor of Bethel Creek, and we'll see where a woman's place is supposed to be." I shook the reins and forged ahead. Bethel Creek was waiting. It had no idea that Wren Birdsong was coming and what else was coming with her.

Or what she would be taking away.

5

THE LIFE I LEFT BEHIND

A funeral cortege wended its way from the house of the bereaved to the First Presbyterian Church. The plain pine coffin was borne inside by an odd assortment of skinny boys and old men who struggled with their task; it seemed that as the influenza epidemic spread, it had decimated the strong more than those with weak constitutions. I watched the procession as I set up my soapbox near Mrs. Cochrane's millinery shop and began to despair that there would be anyone around to hear my speech. It seemed everyone in the village had turned out for the funeral and was filing into the church. I plopped down and stared at my feet, wondering why I had gone to all this trouble when I spotted two other feet toe-to-toe with my own.

"Dearest Wren, I see you have chosen this fine autumn day to make your case to the esteemed citizens of Bethel Creek."

I looked up to see Miss Lanie Lansdale, regaled in white as well, wearing a swooping hat and veil, looking as if she had just stepped from the pages of *Vogue*. Rising, I embraced her and we smiled at one another. "I'm so glad to see someone familiar and friendly," I said, turning to nudge the box closer to the corner of the wooden sidewalk.

"I received your note and would not have missed hearing you for the world."

"I'm afraid no one else will hear me, though." I nodded toward the church.

"Oh, the town is so full of bereavement these days I can scarcely stand it," Miss Lanie said, drawing a lace hanky from her bag and dabbing her eyes. "I have lost four students this week to the vile illness that's going around. Does your mother have any idea why the influenza has suddenly become so deadly?"

I looked at my hands. They were red and chapped from scrubbing laundry, and I wished I had thought to wear gloves, sure that Miss Lanie would notice their condition. "Mother has decided she doesn't want to play town doctor anymore. She's taken to her bed. Not from illness but from some sort of melancholy. I can't shake her from it, and she's left all the responsibilities to me." My voice broke; I turned away so Miss Lanie wouldn't see my tears. She put her silk-gloved hands on my shoulders.

"Dear, dear Wren. We must find some way to free you from this indenture. I fear it is sapping your spirit and strength."

I wiped my eyes and turned to face her. How I longed for the freedom to do as she had done, to look back on the life I left behind with only cool nostalgia and gentle affection.

To take my meager possessions and go someplace where no one knew me, nor I anyone else, and begin anew to forge for myself some identity apart from the suffocation of my ancestry.

"My strength is still here, Miss Lanie. Just an instant of weakness." I spun around for her inspection. "How do I look? I made the dress myself."

She cast an admiring glance and examined the lace trim on the sleeves. "It is fine work. You look stunning. You have a gift and talents for so many things." At that moment the sound of a hymn emanated from the church. "Do you know who has died?"

Shaking my head, I stepped back over to the surrey, where I picked up my purse. "No."

The street was empty now, and there was no point to making a speech to an audience of one, at least not right at this moment.

"Here's an idea," said Miss Lanie. "Why don't we attend the funeral, then afterward we will reconnoiter here and you will make your speech. We'll pay our respects, you'll astound the townspeople afterward with your intelligence and élan, and we will put the town in better spirits than those in which they began the day."

"I don't know," I said. "Maybe the time isn't right, coming immediately after such a solemn occasion as a funeral."

Miss Lanie nodded. "I understand your hesitation. Death and tragedy are constant attendants of our mortal lives—enemies, if you will. When the funeral is concluded, the family will most likely return home to the comfort of those they love and will be oblivious to what goes on outside their walls, at least for a time. The rest of the town will go about its business. They will listen to your speech, Wren. I do not believe anyone will be offended. Life does proceed amidst grief and loss." She held my hands and looked resolutely into my eyes. "So will we make our stand today, dear Wren?"

"So we will."

We set off then to the church; it was nearly full, save a couple of seats in the back, which we took for ourselves. We looked out of place in our white finery and attracted a few glances from snootier folk, but we ignored them and tried to concentrate on the forceful funeral oration being preached by the Reverend Jonas John McKechnie.

Reverend McKechnie was known around town for his fiery sermons, much after the fashion of Jonathan Edwards, whose "Sinners in the Hands of an Angry God" he took as his manifesto for soul salvation. Uncharacteristic for the Presbyterians, he was also known for preaching fire and brimstone at funerals, regardless of how the dearly departed did depart, as either saint or sinner. God may love all, but to Reverend Jonas John McKechnie, the sinner and the saved were going to be preached into the next life in like manner.

"Our brother in Christ has gone on to his reward," he was saying from his spot behind the pulpit. "He was a young man, one unused to the rigors of this world, one unprepared for the plague that has come over our fair town, our great state, our sovereign nation.

"It is a plague!" he shouted, waving his arm in the air, holding his Bible high over his head. "Plagues! God's special punishment for the disobedient, the wicked, and the just alike."

He walked back and forth then, allowing this last to sink in. The grieving family sat in the front row. I could not see their faces, but from time to time I noticed that someone's shoulders shook, or that someone bowed a head and wiped a tear. Glancing around, I noticed several people I knew, including Skeeter Lowe, who also had taken notice of my presence. He angled himself in the pew as to attain a better view of me, and his eyes drilled into me with an expression so inappropriate to the surroundings that I shrank in my seat, trying to hide my face behind Miss Lanie's veil. It was a look I could feel through my pores, and I shivered in spite of the rising heat being produced by the Reverend McKechnie.

"The wrath of God is powerful and all-encompassing." The minister paced across the altar, waving his black leather-bound Bible toward the front row. "Throughout the Holy Word of God we see many examples of how the Almighty has used plagues to return his people to him, and how he punishes the disobedient." He slammed the Bible onto the pulpit and riffled loudly through the pages until he found the passage he sought and read:

"'For I will at this time send all my plagues upon thine heart, and upon thy servants, and upon thy people; that thou mayest know that there is none like me in all the earth.' Exodus 9:14."

He let the words rest on the congregation like holy saw-dust from a newly hewn cross.

"Pharoah hardened his heart, in spite of all of Moses' remonstrations and pleas and warnings. His people were tormented. His people were terrorized. His people were ultimately destroyed. God sent his judgment against the wicked and righteous alike."

To our great discomfiture, he stopped and surveyed each and every person in the congregation. I wanted to stand up and tell him that he should just look at Skeeter, because he had enough wickedness going on in his heart right now to overshadow whatever other wickedness might be on the mind of anyone else present. At that moment, with Rev. McKechnie's eyes boring into our souls, it was a wonder the whole of us didn't stand up and repent on the spot for all the wrongs we hadn't even thought of committing yet.

"Have you ever had a boil?" the preacher asked, almost jovially in tone. "If you have, then you know how painful one boil can be. Can you imagine Job, one righteous man, afflicted with boils over his entire body?" He paused a moment to let the image sink in. "Now can you imagine an entire people, the nation of Egypt, all afflicted with boils to the point that no one could stand before Pharaoh because they were all afflicted. All afflicted!

"God sent frogs, and blood in the water, and gnats and flies, and, boy, don't we know what those are like come August in the humidity and the rain and the heat. He sent a plague that killed their cows, and hail and locusts that destroyed their crops, and finally a plague that killed every firstborn child of Egypt."

Another silence. I glanced over at Skeeter, who was now smiling at me, chewing on a toothpick like some common laborer.

"God curses the disobedient," Reverend McKechnie cried. He came down from the altar and stood behind the coffin, surveying it as if measuring it for himself. Raising his fist, he brought it down on the box and pounded on it as if it were a drum. The sound resonated throughout the chamber, causing some to jump, some to exclaim, and most everyone to rise slightly from their seat.

"'But it shall come to pass, if thou wilt not hearken unto the voice of the LORD thy God, to observe to do all his commandments and his statutes which I command thee this day; that all these curses shall come upon thee, and overtake thee.' Deuteronomy, chapter 28, verse 15." The verse came out in a blur, with the reverend pounding out the punctuation on the coffin, to the congregation's growing dismay. I glanced at Miss Lanie, who watched the scene wide-eyed. "Does everyone in the South get this incensed at a funeral?" she whispered. Someone turned around and shot her a withering look.

The preacher continued quoting. "'Cursed shalt thou be in the city, and cursed shalt thou be in the field.'" *Thump.*

"'Cursed shall be thy basket and thy store.'" *Thump.*

"'Cursed shall be the fruit of thy body, and the fruit of thy land, the increase of thy kine, and the flocks of thy sheep.'" *Thump.*

He went on quoting and thumping until he decided to digress for a moment. "Now our brother here has paid a dear cost for the sins of our brethren."

Everyone in the congregation began surveying one another covertly as if trying to discern the guilty individuals.

"He has reaped the results of the disobedience of a wicked land and a wicked time and a wicked people: 'The LORD shall smite thee with a consumption, and with a fever, and with an inflammation, and with an extreme burning, and with the sword, and with blasting, and with mildew; and they shall pursue thee until thou perish.'"

Reverend McKechnie brought his fist down on the casket.

A sharp cracking sound rent the air.

A man on the front row stood up. "It's split," he said in a loud whisper. "The top of the casket's split clean through."

The poor boy's mother got up, regarded her son's desecrated casket, then walked to the preacher. She grabbed hold of his tie and pulled his face down level with hers.

"You listen here, preacher." Her voice came strong and bold and echoed from the vaulted ceiling. "I brought my boy here to be preached into heaven." You could tell she was spitting out the words because he blinked his eyes and tried to pull back, but she had quite a grip on him. She let go and pointed to the pulpit. "Now you get back up yonder and repeat the Lord's Prayer and let me take my boy out back and bury him. His soul is in God's hands, not your'n."

Reverend McKechnie pulled away, straightened his tie, arranged his face, and walked slowly around back of the pulpit, where he laid down his Bible, quietly, bowed his head, and repeated the prayer. When he finished, the pallbearers got up and took the coffin and bore it to the graveyard behind the sanctuary. Miss Lanie and I compared our consterning thoughts regarding the reverend's outrageous behavior and decided to skip the burying.

We returned to the soapbox and waited. I noticed that Skeeter had skipped the burial as well and had situated himself in a doorway across the street, where he continued to chew on his toothpick. I ignored him and went over my speech in my mind.

"Is he still tormenting you?" Miss Lanie placed her body between us, but when I stepped onto the box, I could still see him over her hat.

"Not bodily, but he's doing his best to torment my spirit today." I looked down at the white dress I had spent so many hours toiling over. Smoothing the skirt, I sought a place inside my mind where Skeeter Lowe didn't matter, didn't exist, was only another bystander wondering what this girl was planning to do on this soapbox.

Skeeter hadn't shared my views on much of anything. Like Mim, he believed a woman's place was in the home, beside her husband, and he could not be swayed. He believed the husband should control the wife—what she wore, whom she spoke with, when she left the house, and where she should go when she did, and certainly accompanied by him. I couldn't see living my life in such a prison. I longed for a union of shared beliefs, shared hopes, shared dreams. Submission to a husband was one thing; there are instances in which a man must submit to the woman's will as well. However, subjugation was another thing entirely, and I refused to become a slave to anyone, man or woman. I already felt the weight of my family's expectations—my fervent desire was to break away and become a woman on my own, a woman free to make her own choices.

A woman, first of all, free to vote.

Mourners from the funeral began milling through the streets. The shop owners who had attended opened their doors to the Saturday crowds. Miss Lanie nodded to me. I stepped onto the box, waiting until people took notice and began gathering around the street corner. As the crowd grew, I was aware of Skeeter grinning at me. I shot him what I thought was a piercing look, then turned my attention to the folks who surrounded me, apparently willing to hear what I had to say. Or at least eager to find out whether the preacher had to worry about any competition from a female orator.

I took a deep breath. Miss Lanie smiled and held up her fists. I nodded.

"Citizens of Bethel Creek," I began, my eyes sweeping over the assembly. "Women of Bethel Creek. I have a message today of great importance and great urgency.

"Our government now has under its consideration a bill that, if passed, would grant the women of our great land, our great state, and our great town the right to stand next to our men and vote our beliefs, to make our voices heard on the issues that affect our families and will affect those who come after us."

Skeeter had worked his way around the edge of the crowd and now stood only about ten feet away, staring at my ankles. I tried not to notice.

"The Nineteenth Amendment to the United States Constitution would grant all women the right to vote. We have

85

earned this right. I submit that women work as hard and as long and as forcefully as any man, and we should have a say in our own governance. Doesn't it make sense that the laws that affect the men of this land also affect the women and children? What if the men with whom we are associated—the fathers, the brothers, the husbands, the sons—do not share our views? Are we not left without a voice in these matters?"

Whispers emanated from the crowd. Miss Lanie lifted her palms toward me. "Keep going," she mouthed.

I straightened my back. A stiff breeze had risen, and my skirt flowed out behind me. I envisioned myself as the figurehead on a massive sailing ship. But a dark cloud was forming over the town—a storm on the horizon. I prayed that if it were going to rain, it would hold off until I finished my speech and collected my accolades.

"Scripture instructs us to render unto God that which is God's, and unto Caesar that which is Caesar's. We have only one true God, who governs us all by divine right. But should we not, as women and citizens of the United States, of South Carolina, and of Bethel Creek, have a say in whom our Caesars might be?"

A loud hoot arose from the far periphery. "I don't remember the Good Book saying anything about picking a Mrs. Caesar." The crowd began to laugh.

"Yeah," came a reply from the other side. "Last time I looked, when you paid Mr. Caesar, Mrs. Caesar was the one who got a new hat and shoes!"

Miss Lanie came up beside me. "Don't let them distract you, Wren," she whispered fiercely. "You are making your point. You notice no women are heckling you. Only men."

My legs trembled—I wasn't sure how much longer I could stand there, but I had to finish. I wanted Miss Lanie to be proud. I wanted the women of Bethel Creek to be proud. I wanted to prove that a woman could have her say and that men would listen and truly understand her point of view. Perhaps it was naiveté on my part. I looked at my feet for a moment. Then I threw my head back, smiled directly at the hecklers, and began again in a steady, clear voice. At least I hoped it was clear.

"If you will recall your history, dear sirs, you will remember that Caesar fought a war just to make Cleopatra a queen, a sovereign ruler over all Egypt. All we are asking is that you allow us the vote so we may choose our mayor, our governor, and our president."

At this, some women in the crowd cheered, while others looked at me with blank stares, and still others shook their heads. It was obvious the women needed as much convincing as the men.

A low rumble rolled through the still air. The storm was drawing near, and the crowd began to disperse.

"Please write to your leaders—your congressman and your senator—and ask that they support this bill, that they give the female citizens of our land the ability to cast the vote, so that we may stand on equal footing and make our voices heard. God bless you and thank you."

A couple of people applauded, among them Miss Lanie, who had taken off her gloves so the sound would echo throughout the emptying street. I stepped down from the box and picked it up.

"Wren, you were fabulous," she gushed, kissing me on the cheek. "I am so proud of you."

"I believe you would have gotten far more attention and respect."

"My dear, I am an outsider. They would have heckled me far worse than they did you. I believe they showed remarkable restraint because of your family's station in this county."

"You mean they showed remarkable tolerance and condescension. You didn't see their faces."

I walked back to the surrey and put the box in the backseat. Miss Lanie followed, chattering all the while.

"I could feel their mood, Wren. They showed great respect by simply standing there and listening to you. You showed intelligence, knowledge, even a biting wit."

"Do you think I changed anyone's mind?"

"You have planted the seeds of an idea in their heads. The change will come later when they sit down to reflect on your words and thoughts."

I was heartened by this last and told her so. We said our good-byes—I still had to shop for our household supplies—and she returned to the school. I went over to the general store, where I bought the goods we needed, and to the post office for the mail. Then, reluctantly, I got into the surrey for the ride home.

A slow, thrumming rain began that subdued my mood further. As I was pushing Jake along the road, an automobile came from the opposite direction. A man in uniform occupied the front passenger seat. Charley came to mind. I wondered what he was doing now that he was in camp, if being there and preparing for war had made any difference in his feelings regarding the same.

It was one reason I wanted the vote. So I would have a say in who would send my men to war.

A sound distinct from the thunder roared from behind me, startling Jake, who laid back his ears and bellowed. Both sounds startled me. Presently, a car passed the surrey and stopped ahead of us. Skeeter Lowe jumped out. I pulled to a halt, but Jake wouldn't stand still. He nipped at Skeeter's shoulder as he passed by. Skeeter feigned a punch at the mule.

"Don't you dare touch him," I scolded. "What are you doing?"

"Just decided I'd follow you home and make sure you're all right." He propped a foot on the step and pulled out a cigarette. He leaned his head into the surrey, his face close to mine as he lit it, out of the rain. The smoke clouded the air, and I pulled my head away.

"I'm perfectly fine, and I don't need you checking on me. Now if you'll get back in your car . . ."

"After hearing your little talk, I thought you might like for me to teach you how to drive." He drew on the cigarette and blew the smoke away this time. "Seems a woman who wants to vote ought to want to drive an automobile, too."

I thought about it for a moment. Skeeter made me nervous, yes, but I so wanted to learn how to drive. The growing epidemic had delayed the delivery of Miss Lanie's automobile, and someone would have to teach her to drive when it arrived, before she could even think about teaching me. And there was no telling when Charley would return to Bethel Creek. Skeeter now confined his gaze to my face.

"I'm not going to hurt you, Wren," he said.

"You've hurt me in many ways in the past. You're supposed to stay away from me."

He put his hand lightly around my wrist. "Haven't I shown restraint? Haven't I given you time to think about what you want out of this life? I didn't heckle you back there like those other men, did I?"

"No, you didn't. But the way you were looking at me, I could tell you were thinking about it."

"You could tell, huh. Let me tell you—I believed in what you were saying, Wren. I didn't know what a gem I had when I had you. I was stupid, treating you the way I did." Letting go of my arm, he took a few more drags off the cigarette before flicking it onto the ground and grinding it out with his boot heel. Then he held out his hand. "Let's go for a ride, Wren. I promise it'll be fun."

"I can't," I replied, my resolve weakening. The way Skeeter spoke, so softly, the way he touched my arm, so gently. "They're expecting me at home. I have the supplies . . ."

"The supplies can wait. Ol' Jake here'll be all right by the road for a few minutes. We can hitch him to that tree yonder. Besides, it's drier in my car."

He looked at me with such innocence. It reminded me of how he was when we were children, when he treated me like his friend.

"Just a short distance," I said, shaking the reins and steering Jake toward the tree. Skeeter followed at a trot and tied up the old mule, who tried to take another nip out of him.

"Feisty ol' critter today, aren't you?" said Skeeter. He took me by the hand and led me toward the car. "Now you just sit in here and watch what I do. Then in a little bit we'll switch, and you can try. Not a thing to it."

I got in and adjusted my skirts around me. I really hadn't wanted to go home yet—back to that kitchen and those stares and those endless expectations. Skeeter cranked the car and we set off, soon coming to a side road that I had somehow failed to notice in all my years of travel between home and Bethel Creek.

"Where does this lead? I've never been back here before."

Skeeter grinned. "Fishing spot. Not many folks know about it. It's kind of a secret. When we get down there, we'll switch places, and you can drive us back."

The sky grew darker, the rain heavier. It was getting harder to see the thin trail ahead of us. "Skeeter, I think we should go back." I started to tremble and tried to think of some excuse. "It's getting slippery, and I shouldn't leave the surrey or Jake out in the weather so long."

Skeeter didn't reply. He just kept driving, and he started smiling that smile, that scary smile, the one that made me feel like I was sitting there in just my feminine garments. My scalp crawled. Suddenly I felt cold, though the day was humid and oppressive, the way it feels before a cool front blows through and cleans the air.

The river came into view. Skeeter stopped the car. I guessed we were about a mile, maybe more, from the main road. All I could hear were the sounds of the river rushing by, the rain beating on the roof of the car. I started to open the door so I could get out and rush around to the driver's seat.

Skeeter reached over me. Snatched my hand from the door handle. Slammed the door.

"You don't want to get that pretty white dress all wet, do you?" He stroked the folds of my skirt with one hand as he draped the other around my shoulders. I pulled the skirt closer around me. "Let's wait a bit until it slacks, then we can switch and you can drive us back."

He leaned in until I could feel his breath, hot and reeking of tobacco, against my cheek. My hair tightened against my scalp, and I realized he was pulling my head backwards so he could lay his disgusting lips against my throat.

I felt him rip my dress.

Rain blew through the cracked-open windows, which fogged as I fought against his coarse hands, hands that felt slimy and cold and disgusting.

I tried to speak, but he strangled my words, and I was forced to silence.

Then he forced me to submission.

He took it away. At that moment, Skeeter Lowe took away everything I wanted in life. He took away my hopes, my dreams. He took away the sacred part of me that be-longed to the unknown man who would become my husband someday. He took away a part of my heart that God gave me for the purpose of love. In the midst of that terrible struggle, in my mind, in my soul, I cried out to God.

God did not answer.

In a moment when he allowed me to breathe, I screamed with all my might into that lonesome place where he had taken me, where I had put my own desires ahead of good sense, where my body and soul were paying the cost of a small wish. I screamed with all my might again and again until someone opened the door of the car and a hand reached in.

That hand held a rock, a rock that smashed against Skeeter's head, causing blood to rush from a wound, blood that joined other blood that soiled my dress of purest white, and he fell away.

I got out and ran until I fell. I thought I heard voices behind me, but I didn't turn around, afraid that Skeeter was coming after me, that he was going to kill me next. Two hands lifted me and stood me on the muddy road, which by now seemed ten miles long, and pulled me along until we reached the surrey. There Thracia Mills put me on the seat, untied Jake from the tree, and drove me as fast as the old mule would trot toward my home, the place I had longed to escape this morning, which I now sought as a refuge I might never leave again.

Thracia never said a word or made a sound. She never even looked me in the eyes.

She just saved me.

We were both drenched to the skin and filthy. Mud caked around our ankles and the bottoms of our skirts. Her long black hair was plastered to her back. Skeeter's blood was caked on her hands, but she didn't seem to notice.

"Where did you come from?" I managed to whisper. My throat hurt; I could barely speak.

She didn't answer, and I was too weary to press her. I had never seen Thracia speak to anyone, and I guess she didn't plan to start then.

The rain slackened as we approached my house. When we pulled up, no one came out, none of the boys, to take the surrey and Jake into the barn. "Go into the house and get my mother," I said. I was shaking so badly that I didn't think I could walk.

Thracia stood in the rain and stared at me before taking my arm.

"I said for you to go into the house and get my mother." I tried to scream it, but my vocal cords refused to work. The words broke into individual letters I don't think anyone would have understood.

Instead she kept standing in the rain, with water sheeting off her indigo-hued hair, forming a puddle behind her feet. Finally I realized I was going to have to walk into the house in my ripped, filthy, bloody dress and face whoever was there, face more humiliation, face the fact that nothing would ever be the same, that like Miss Lanie, I had now left my old life behind for an unknown destiny, and my steps now would be the first ones I would take into that treacherous future.

Thracia took my arm and helped me from the surrey, up the steps and into the kitchen where everyone sat around the table. Mother sat on the floor, with her head lying on the seat of Papa's chair. No one noticed our arrival but Micah, who got up and came to me, not seeing my destruction, looking only into my eyes.

"Some men came, Wren," he said. He started to put his hands on my shoulders, but I backed away and he put his hands down to his sides. I looked around the room and realized everyone—all of my brothers, and my mother—was crying. "Charley's dead."

I couldn't understand what he was saying. It didn't make sense. Charley was at training camp. Soldiers didn't die in training camps. They died in battle. Charley hadn't left for Europe yet, probably wouldn't leave for another couple of months.

"He died of the influenza, Wren," Micah was saying, as my brothers sat in shock and my mother grieved the loss of her firstborn son.

My voice returned then, for a moment. "Charley's dead," I repeated, before grabbing Thracia and fainting onto the hard kitchen floor.

6

THE SPANISH LADY

No one ever said the word. Rape wasn't something a woman talked about, much less admitted when it happened to her. It was a reason for shame, for shunning. A woman knew better than to admit something so terrible had happened to her, lest she be branded by all—men and women—for somehow bringing it on herself, while the perpetrator went on about his daily life as if nothing had happened.

I hoped that Skeeter was dead, but I knew the world didn't work that way. It would be too simple. He had done a terrible thing to me, and I felt—I knew—I was partly to blame. Vanity, pride, an innocent desire, my own ambition, all had been my undoing.

Now my oldest brother—the one I looked to for guidance, for protection, for cheer, one of the brothers I loved best—was taken away.

No one found out that Skeeter had raped me because I told no one. I certainly didn't have to worry about Thracia telling anyone. Everyone thought I had fainted from grief. I had. But it was a two-headed sorrow, and I let them think it was the one rather than admit the humiliation of the other. When I recovered from my faint, Thracia was the one who took me to my room, cleaned me up, and put me to bed. Everyone was too struck down with grief, it seemed, to notice anything out of the ordinary about Thracia's sudden presence within our home.

It turned out to be only the beginning of changes that no one could have foreseen.

Mother spent her days mourning the loss of her firstborn son. Inwardly, I was glad that she had not heard Reverend McKechnie's admonitions, else she might have displayed a tendency of Mim's and become convinced straight off that our family was under some kind of curse. She had prepared herself to lose her son in war and had even spoken of the possibility in most cavalier terms. She had not expected to lose her son to illness, so quickly, so easily, to something as common as influenza.

Through a fog I watched her mourn, and I mourned doubly, the loss of my innocence and the loss of my eldest brother. I thought to tell her what had befallen me on that rainy afternoon, at the hands of a man Mim thought I should marry, but I could not catch a break in her overpowering sorrow. Similarly, my brothers withdrew from us and from one another and all of them mooned around the place, seeking isolation where little was to be found.

Compounding this was the incessant stream of people who came to our doorway, either to express their condolences for our loss or to implore us to help hold off impending griefs of their own. It seemed half the town had fallen ill, and no one knew what to do, where the plague had come from, how to treat it. Mother refused to speak to anyone, and I was forced from my own bed of misery the next day to deal with these desperate folk, to administer my mother's remedies as best I could, and to hide the feeling that I needed to scream until I had no voice, no sound, no sadness left.

Through it all, Thracia became a silent presence in our home. I had not invited her to stay, and Mother failed to notice that once she had arrived home with me, she didn't bother leaving.

And Thracia watched us all. I began to wonder which was worse, having been watched by Skeeter or having Thracia trace my every move and action with those black eyes and that steady gaze.

I had to give it to her. She worked. Seeming to sense my weakness and my mother's emotional absence, she cooked and cleaned and washed and fed and chopped wood and did whatever we needed with a vigor one would never have suspected, as all she ever seemed to do before was stand around and observe whatever passed directly in front of her eyes. I had never imagined she could do so much, given the most activity I had ever seen from her was leaning against posts and chewing licorice.

When Charley's body was brought home a couple of days later, I tried to think of some way to avoid going to the funeral. He was my brother and I loved him dearly, but I was too ashamed of what had happened to me. As long as I stayed under my roof, no one could see my face or seek to discern the trial I had undergone.

And on the heels of Charley's coffin came a man from the government—the United States Public Health Service, in fact. Jeremiah heralded his arrival, screaming and running into the parlor as if Frankenstein's monster had materialized on our front porch.

His name was Dr. Connell Redmond, and he wore a surgical mask. For the first few minutes of his visit, he hunkered down, speaking quietly to Jeremiah, who had hidden his face in my skirt and refused to lay eyes on this strange man. Finally, Dr. Redmond gave up trying to soothe my poor brother's fright and turned his attention to me. I'll admit it was disconcerting to speak to someone whose full facial expression you couldn't see. I kept my distance as he spoke. He seemed to note this and stayed outside the doorway.

"I apologize for the mask," he said, tugging it over his chin. "It's a necessary precaution for those of us in the public health profession. We don't want to be accused of spreading the very illness the health service has charged us with preventing."

"What is your business?" I turned my head to the side, and it was then that Dr. Redmond seemed to note the coffin in our parlor and Mother's quiet conversation with the undertaker.

"I apologize. It's obvious your family has suffered a loss, as have so many others in your fair county." He fumbled with his hat. "Are you Mrs. Huldah Birdsong? Several townspeople told me that she's the closest thing Bethel Creek has to a physician here."

"No, I am not. I'm Wren Birdsong—Miss Birdsong to you. My mother is greatly grieved. I don't believe she's up to any more visitors right now. The epidemic took my oldest brother, and the townspeople will not give us rest to mourn because of the illnesses of their own loved ones. As you can imagine, we have been inundated."

"That is one reason I have come to see her, to explain the restrictions everyone must now observe to contain this epidemic."

"Restrictions?" I pried Jeremiah from my leg and told him to go into the kitchen where he would find a plate full of freshly baked tea cakes.

"Would you like to step outside where we can talk, Miss Birdsong?"

I glanced at Mother, who hadn't even noticed our conversation, and stepped onto the porch, where I again kept a distance of a few feet between myself and Dr. Redmond. Thracia was standing in the hallway, watching us, so I closed the front door.

Dr. Redmond removed his mask completely then. I was struck by the fact that he appeared only a few years older than me. He sounded to be a man much older, although I supposed what with all that was going on, anyone's voice could age in tandem. His hands were large, with graceful but strong fingers; his hair was black, and he had a strong chin and steady eyes, although his overall demeanor was somewhat shy.

"Is it safe for you to remove that?" I asked, indicating the mask, which was now sticking out of his coat pocket.

"Out-of-doors it's generally all right to remove it. We think the illness seems to spread more rapidly in enclosed spaces." From his other pocket, he removed a brochure and handed it to me. I looked at it, but I confess that I could not even read the words. I was exhausted to the point of near blindness and went over to the porch swing where I sat and pretended I knew what I was looking at.

Still, he wasn't fooled.

"Miss Birdsong, you look a little flushed. May I . . . ?" He reached into his bag, which he had placed on the porch banister, pulled out a thermometer, and approached me.

"You may not." My expression must have told him to back away, for that is what he did.

He cleared his throat. "Well, then, what I came by to explain to your mother was that we need someone in each community to act as a public health officer to carry out our guidelines for stemming the spread of this influenza."

"How is she to do that?" I continued to look at the brochure although the words blurred before my eyes. I finally made out the title: *Spanish Influenza*. Not thinking clearly, I wondered what Spain had to do with the flu outbreak.

"It's all right there," he replied, pointing to the paper, which I let fall into my lap.

Somehow my mind perceived that I needed it to function. "I need you to explain it to me, in case it's not all in the brochure."

"Specifically, we need someone to make sure that all places where public gatherings occur are closed for the duration—churches, schools, theaters. I've already spoken with the mayor and council, but they seem reluctant to enforce such closures."

"Perhaps they're afraid it will affect business," I said, stating the obvious.

"If the epidemic spreads, there may be no business to be had." He paused for a moment to let that sink in.

"Is it really that bad?"

"Elsewhere in the country it is. This epidemic is wiping out entire households. The army camps are full of it."

I couldn't process what he was saying.

He went on with practical matters. "Everyone who goes out in public should wear a mask such as the one I have on—a lady in each household should be charged with making them for her family."

100

I held my tongue and looked at a point just over Dr. Redmond's shoulder. This seemed to rattle him, but he continued anyway.

"If the town does not have an ordinance against spitting, perhaps Mrs. Birdsong could encourage the council to enact one."

"An ordinance against what?"

"Spitting."

"Spitting?"

"Spitting. Like tobacco juice, which is also a harmful habit. The ordinance should be expedited and enforced."

I would have laughed, but it would have taken energy I didn't have that particular moment.

"Spitting spreads germs through the salivary juices. We need Mrs. Birdsong to distribute pamphlets throughout the county on how to contain the epidemic's spread."

"What of those who don't know how to read? Many of our neighbors are illiterate."

"Then perhaps she—or you—could explain the contents of the brochure to them."

I found myself slowly squeezing the brochure into a ball. A fatigue deeper than I had ever known ran through my body, and I wanted to crawl under my warm quilts and sleep for days, weeks, until all this pain, this hurt, this grief, this incessant talking, stopped.

"Also, we need someone to prepare daily, weekly, and monthly reports, which they will send to our statisticians in Washington, who will compile information that can help us determine further courses of action."

At this point, I finally focused in on his eyes. They were the color of jade. I had never seen eyes that color. At any other time I would have found it fascinating. Here I found it only a curiosity that took my mind away from my fatigue and pain and the knowledge that only two other people knew what had happened to me, one of whom was probably going on with his daily life as if nothing had happened.

"Oh, and I think it would be advisable if your family held a private burial rather than a public funeral."

At that point I noticed that Mother had opened the door and was listening to our conversation. Her eyes looked as if they were going to leap from their sockets, and her skin flamed in spite of the crisp autumn day. She came out and pointed to the car, which Dr. Redmond had apparently borrowed from someone in town. It looked familiar.

"Dear sir, I do not know who gave you the authority to deny citizens the right to mourn those whom they have loved," she said, "but I would invite you to leave my property this instant."

Now I felt sorry for Dr. Redmond. He was only doing his job, after all, and here my mother, Mrs. Huldah Birdsong, had picked this moment to come back to herself and resume her former rude ways, with him as her first victim.

He didn't even flinch. "Mrs. Birdsong, I believe this is necessary to stop the spread of the epidemic. Surely you do not want other mothers to suffer your same grief, to mourn the loss of a firstborn son?"

Mother watched him for a moment, arms akimbo, looking much like her old self for a moment. "No, sir, and neither would I deny them—any of them—the right to a proper funeral attended by family and friends who would wish to mourn their loved one's departure."

"Then I would suggest that you keep the casket closed."

At this, Mother's face went beyond crimson. I felt an urge to duck underneath the porch swing and let it bang me on the head. It would surely be less painful than what Dr. Redmond was about to endure.

"You would deny a mother a last look at her son? The last time she should behold his countenance this side of heaven? You would deny this to a mother? You would deny this to the woman who bore the pain of his birth, who raised him through fat times and lean, and who loved and adored him to the very core of his being, as she does her other children? You would deny this?"

I realized I was holding my breath. I had been doing that a lot, ever since my father disappeared from our home. Dr. Redmond appeared to be doing the same. Unfortunately, Mother was just getting started.

"Dear doctor, you need to go back to your fancy medical school and get yourself a better grounding in bedside manner. If you are going to stride throughout the countryside advising the citizenry on how to stem this epidemic, then you had better be prepared to encounter a tidal wave of grief. You had better be ready to withstand the evil day, because what you are suggesting will surely produce more anger, more grief, more evil than any death surely would. Women have the right to mourn their young. Even a cat will search for a dead kitten taken away and buried. Even cats can count, Dr. Redmond. You would deny a human mother, a mother blessed by our dear Lord and Father in heaven with the gift of a child, of children with whom he entrusts us, you would deny us the right to bid our loved one farewell in private and the right to grieve publicly? Sir, you have no business in the medical profession." She snatched a brochure from his hand and tore it in to shreds. "Or is this why they have sent you about the country handing out tracts instead of putting you to work at the profession for which some expensive university has allegedly trained you?"

Mother spun on her heel, walked back into the house, and slammed the door, leaving us to stare at one another.

Even I had never heard Mother get so wound up. I pitied the poor undertaker who had wisely chosen to cower in the parlor. Even Thracia had the good sense to disappear.

"Is your mother always so . . . so . . ."

"Outspoken?"

"Yes. Yes, outspoken is an appropriate description."

I had to smile, although I'm afraid it was without warmth. I had felt nothing but a chill ever since . . . "I'm afraid she was more so than usual. You must forgive her." I went to the porch railing, where he had laid a stack of brochures held together by a rubber band, and took some. "I'll take these. I'll wind up handing them out anyway."

"Thank you, Miss Birdsong." He smiled and held out his hand, but I backed away. His smile faded. "Are you sure you're all right?"

"No, Dr. Redmond, I am not all right" I replied, lowering my eyes. "My brother is dead, remember?"

He started down the steps. "I'll be staying in town a few days, traveling to various outposts. Would it be okay if I came by another day—perhaps after your brother is buried?"

I shrugged. "If you like. I doubt Mother will be any kinder."

"I don't wish to see your mother. I think someone needs to see about you."

I looked into his eyes then and wondered if it was that obvious, if my pain and violation were that transparent. But he couldn't know. There was no way he could know. No physician in my experience had ever been that perceptive. Mother could not read my mind. How could a stranger?

He left then without saying anything else, and I gave no reply, not even a wave.

It was all too much. I sank onto the steps and cried until the tears soaked my handkerchief and then my apron.

The sun set, and the chill of night added to my own, and I wondered if I would ever feel warm again.

In defiance of Dr. Redmond's request, Mother ordered that Charley's coffin should remain open until his funeral. I couldn't stand to see the face of my dear brother, taken so young. He was dressed in his army uniform, so distinguished—he would have made a fine soldier, would have led his men in battle, would have been victorious because of his beliefs and patriotism. I looked at him for only a few brief moments, after which I avoided the parlor.

The rest of my brothers couldn't seem to tear themselves away. Teddy, Wilson, Micah, Nehemiah, and Jeremiah kept Mother company as she kept vigil. They were all silent; the entire house was the quietest it had ever been. It was almost a relief, but I didn't dare say it out loud.

I wanted so to talk to someone about what had happened to me; I searched my mind for someone I could turn to. The most obvious choice was Miss Lanie, but given her feelings about Skeeter, I was afraid she would do something rash.

Should I go to the sheriff? Surely not. He would not take me seriously. A rape charge was very serious—I would be on trial more so than Skeeter. Should I speak to the minister? I was too ashamed to speak of such things with a man of God.

God, our Father who art in heaven.

I could not hallow his name. At some point during the rain, between the screams and the struggling and the fighting back to no avail, it was as if God left me. I sincerely believed it. I no longer felt him in my heart or soul. My cries for help, my silent prayers for Skeeter to stop, had

105

gone unanswered. I felt desolation where before I felt solace—peace. I lost not only a precious gift entrusted to me. I lost my faith, my hopes, my dreams, my desires. It was as if my soul had died, only I had no casket in which to bury it, no rites with which to mourn it.

At the First Methodist Church, our minister gave Charley a solemn eulogy, one of proper verses, with proper hymns and appropriate sentiments. At the grave, we buried Charley, and as each of my brothers tossed a handful of soil onto his coffin while it was lowered, I imagined myself a requiem for all the sorrows I now bore, sorrows I would bear in silence, in rage, in private.

I had dressed in black that morning, swathing my face in veils to hide myself from the eyes of Bethel Creek. I could not wear white again, would not—it was another loss. I would not walk down the aisle in white, and Charley was not here to give me away to the man I would someday marry, if I could ever bring myself to love a man in the way women do.

If I only knew, if I could only have had an inkling of what was to come, perhaps I would have thrown myself in the grave with my brother. Because what happened next only aggravated the wounds and made me wish that there really were such a thing as heaven. Wish. If only I could have believed.

7

COFFIN FITS

All interest in aviation halted—the plans for a homemade airplane were put away in a drawer with the old linens to rot. My brothers drifted in and out of the house like shadows. Micah, my one solace, the one brother other than Charley with whom I could hold an intelligent conversation, withdrew not only from the outside world but from our family as well. I couldn't even coax him from his bedroom. He spent his days staring out the window at a world he couldn't bring himself to walk through.

I so wished I had a sister. I needed another woman to talk to about the broken places of my heart, about all I had lost. But no one was there except Thracia, with her looks and stares. I wondered sometimes just what she comprehended of life in our house, where she had made herself at home with neither invitation nor reproach. Mother hadn't asked her to leave, to my surprise, but then Mother had never been one to turn away strangers, much less strange benefactors. Dr. Redmond being the exception.

I withdrew as well. I no longer had the heart for being a suffragette. Skeeter destroyed that dream with the first rip of my beautiful white dress. Although I still wanted to flee Bethel Creek, I now saw it as a way to leave behind what had happened to me, to avoid the reality that Skeeter Lowe was still alive and well, walking the streets with his evil heart intact while mine ached with shame and loneliness.

For her part, Mother, who had let the death of our neighbors put her to bed, now revived and was absent nearly all the time, attending to the growing numbers of townspeople who had fallen ill with the influenza. She did not ask me to accompany her on these expeditions, choosing instead to run herself into the ground each day, dragging in each night after dark to a cold supper and often falling into her bed fully dressed. I suppose it was her way of dealing with her grief. Mourning by exhaustion, which may not have been a bad way.

The one time in my life I would have liked to confide in my mother, she became an even bigger specter than my father. I loved Mother, but she had always treated me as if I were some kind of extension of her. I felt that in her absence, I should *be* her. Only I couldn't do it anymore.

So it was in the midst of all this distance-putting between us all that tragedy began to insert itself on a large scale.

Jeremiah was the first. One evening he came up to me as I was mending a shirt for Wilson. He leaned his head against my arm, watching my stitches, and when I reached over to tousle his beautiful blond hair I noticed that he was sweating profusely. I pulled his head up, looked into his precious face, and saw that he was falling ill, and at a rapid pace. I gathered him into my arms, yelled for Thracia, who appeared from somewhere in the house, and we bounded up the stairs into the boys' room. I undressed Jeremiah and placed him in his little bed. We washed him with cool, wet cloths, but his fever would not lessen. After a while, he began to cough. His lips turned purple. I went out into the shed and plundered Mother's remedies, searching for something that would stop the progress of his illness.

Yet I knew it was hopeless. Too many people had died already, and I knew no remedy could subdue this enemy. Once the lips began to turn, the end was coming and nothing could stop it. I wandered through Mother's Garden of Eden, shivering against the night air, my stomach churning, wishing I could believe in miracles again.

It was as if Reverend McKechnie's sermon had been a prophecy and Dr. Redmond's warnings a confirmation of it. As the epidemic reached its height, the influenza struck at will, with no discernable pattern, no means of prevention, no method of treatment.

I had distributed the brochures, as Dr. Redmond requested, but even with my explanations concerning hygiene, no one seemed to think the measures would do any good. The churches did cease services, and the schools closed—ministers were spending their time preaching to the die-hard converts, and the schools were so empty, the teachers would have had to repeat themselves to cover all the lessons for all the children.

As an example, I wore my face mask whenever I went about, but Mother scoffed at my poor efforts at containment, so I eventually gave it up. It was hot and uncomfortable; I felt as if I were suffocating. A few people kept wearing them, the truly fearful, but as time wore on and the capriciousness of the illness became apparent, folks became aware that nothing would stop the spread.

Horror stories were rampant. The influenza decimated entire families. Parents took to scattering their children to various relatives so that, perhaps, a child might survive. Folk remedies were invented to deal with the outbreak. We heard a story from out West about a woman who covered her child with raw onions to protect her from getting the virus. It worked. Many people started eating raw onions, much as you would an apple, every day. Pretty soon, the town grocer ran out of onions.

The aroma of the town became enough to kill a body. If it wasn't the ingestion of onions, it was the wearing of garlic bulbs or asafetida bags. You would have thought the stench would have been enough to kill the virus.

It wasn't, though. In family after family, house after house, people died—old, young, Negro, white, rich, poor. Whether the sick were attended by a physician, the family matriarch, or the only person who managed to escape infection, the death rate rose in spite of all efforts, futile and heroic.

I didn't want to go back into the house because I was afraid of what I would see when I returned. Jason Spurley again, the blood against the white pillowcase, the darkened skin like a mummy. Thracia came down the steps and motioned for me to come inside.

"Why don't you talk?" I said, continuing to pace. "You know how that puts people off, you not talking all the time. Don't you have words in those lungs of yours? Don't you have words in that brain?"

She continued to watch me, pulling her shawl around her shoulders. I walked toward her and put my face close to hers. She reeked of the cabbage she had cooked for supper that night—the smell made my stomach churn even more. I stared directly into her eyes, but she didn't blink. The moon shone down on us both until a cloud passed over it.

Jeremiah cried out. Then the night was silent. I ran inside and up the stairs, where I found my other brothers gathered around him. I pushed my way through and fell on my knees next to the bed.

"He's dead, Wren," said Micah before turning to leave. His voice was flat, his face blank. I heard the door to his room close quietly.

"Why didn't you do something for him, Wren?" Teddy asked, glaring at me and Thracia. He put his hands on my shoulders and started shaking me. "You weren't supposed to let him die! Why didn't you stop him from dying, Wren?"

"I tried. There's not much we can do for this." I put my hands over my face.

"Then why didn't Mother do anything?" Teddy asked. "She knows how to heal people."

"She doesn't know how to heal people. She only knows how to treat them. And in case you haven't noticed, she isn't here." I rose and covered Jeremiah's face with the sheet as tears rolled down my face. I was so tired, so tired. "Get out," I whispered.

"He's our brother," Teddy said, folding his arms and taking a defiant pose. "We're staying until you go get the undertaker."

I looked at my brothers, who looked back at me as I knew they would, as if I were the parent and they were the children.

"He's my brother, too, you know. He died under my care, but I don't expect you to understand that. Now get out of here and find the undertaker." My voice rose. "Find Mother if you can. Go house to house if you have to, and you tell her that her Jeremiah's gone." I was screaming by this point. My brothers ran from the room as much from fear as demand.

Thracia had disappeared again, thankfully, and I was left to mourn my baby brother alone. I sank to my knees and tried to think of a prayer, the Lord's Prayer, a psalm, any prayer, but none came. It was as if I had lost all of God's words, although Mother and Papa had drilled them into my mind since I was old enough to speak. So I stared at the form made by the sheet with a blank mind, a mind that couldn't comprehend that I had now lost two of my brothers, that I could no longer summon the Lord, whose blessings now seemed like curses.

The boys couldn't find Mother. So I stayed there for what seemed like hours until they returned with the undertaker. I was forced to arrange the burial of my brother alone.

"Can any of your brothers build a coffin?" Mr. Derwin asked.

"I thought you sold coffins."

"So many people are dying that I've run clean out," he replied, placing Jeremiah's body in the back of his hearse. "Folks are having to build their own if they want the body buried proper."

I hadn't planned on this, and I watched the road, hoping for Mother's return. "If that's what you need, I'll see if I can get Wilson and Teddy to build one."

"Very well." Mr. Derwin climbed onto the hearse. "I'll get the body ready as soon as possible."

He drove away before I could object to his calling Jeremiah "the body." I felt light-headed and went inside, where I sat at the table until I became so weary that I decided to put my head down for a moment. I fell asleep.

When I awoke, it was daylight. Mother was sitting at the other end of the table, sipping coffee, looking about two feet away from the grave herself.

"Your father should have told you to go to bed," she said, and I knew right away she was unaware of what had happened. "I must tell him to look after you better when I'm called away."

"Papa's gone, Mother." I rose from the table and walked to the other end, where I stood looking almost directly at the top of her head. "Papa's been gone for years. Just as Charley is gone, and now Jeremiah."

"Jeremiah?" She laughed. *She laughed.* "He's fast asleep upstairs, as are your other brothers."

"No, he's not." I fought to control my voice. The smell of coffee nauseated me, so I stepped back. "Jeremiah caught the flu and none of us noticed. He died last night. Mr. Derwin took him away."

She dropped the cup onto the table; it broke, and coffee ran onto the floor, where Titania and Tiberius sampled it with tentative pink tongues.

Mother stood and took my chin into her palm before slapping me so hard that I lost my balance and fell against the pie safe.

"Do not lie to me about my children." Her voice was steady and frightening.

"*Your* children. Then why do they feel so much more like my own?" I pushed her, something I shouldn't have done, for then she struck me with her fist. I fell to the floor.

"I bore you all, and you have no right to lie to me and tell me a child of mine is dead when I know he is still alive."

I rubbed my stinging cheek. "Go upstairs and look in his room. Ask the boys. They had to go get the undertaker because neither our mother nor our father was here to do it." I pulled myself up and sat on a bench, where I leaned over and held my stomach.

Mother watched me for a moment, then went upstairs. At first the sounds were subdued, like conversation, before turning to yells and screams that pierced the air like sewing needles through fabric until I thought my ears would bleed. After a while she stumbled back into the kitchen, wearing a dumbfounded expression. She paced around the room.

"Where is your father? I must tell your father." She kept repeating these words to herself until finally I rose and took her by the shoulders and shook her.

"Papa is not here. He hasn't been here for three years. He hardly knew Jeremiah. Papa's gone. He might as well be dead, too."

She shrugged my hands from her shoulders and backed away, one expression fading off, another fading on. Her face suddenly looked as it would on an ordinary day, and her voice came out in a normal pitch. "I need to wash and change my dress. I have many patients to attend to today, Wren."

"Mother, Jeremiah is dead!" I cried. "We have to bury him. Mr. Derwin doesn't even have a casket. The boys will have to make one."

Mother looked straight through me then, not seeing her daughter, just someone whose words she did not want to hear. I think I knew that it was useless. I think I finally realized that my mother was deranged. All I could do now was handle things myself. The boys, the house, the task of burying my baby brother—it was all up to me.

If she only knew how close I came to going crazy myself at that moment. How fervently I wished that Papa would come home and make us a family again. But as she often told me, if wishes were horses, beggars would ride. I knew then to wish for anything was useless. Or to hope. Or to pray.

Because I realized then that no one was listening.

My brothers died, one by one, rapid, dreadful deaths that I could not comprehend even as I watched it happen. At a certain point, I believe I became as detached as Mother, and refused to see what was happening before my very eyes. Wilson went next, then Nehemiah, followed by Teddy. Finally, Micah fell away. Micah, who had become so severely locked in his own world that he had forgotten he was put here to live. Now it was too late.

I nursed them through to their deaths, trying every treatment Mother had ever dreamed up. Mim and the sisters sent word that they had quarantined themselves and would not attend so much as a funeral. I needed their help, but at least they would speak to me, something Mother no longer did and something Thracia was either unable or unwilling to do. Our house became silent, save for the coughing and misery that typified this illness.

Dr. Connell Redmond returned to our home the day Micah passed away. His mission had taken him throughout the county, and he had been pressed into service, trying to help the many patients Mother could not attend to. As with Mother, his many nostrums had failed, and he was weary and perplexed. I noticed that he, too, had given up his surgical mask.

I had been up with Micah all night, pressing cool cloths against his darkening skin, watching the inevitable decline that I now knew too intimately. Mother's shadow passed the door around 3:00 A.M. It was as if she had decided that she had no family, that she could bear the loss better if she simply divorced herself from what was going on and treated us all as if we belonged to someone else.

Thracia spelled me at Micah's side. How we escaped the illness ourselves, I didn't know, given our close exposure. When Dr. Redmond visited that morning, I was sitting on the front porch, breathing in a welcome fall breeze. I felt feverish and nauseated, but I attributed it to a lack of food and sleep and the unexpressed grief that weighed on my heart, for I hadn't had time to grieve. As each of my brothers died, there was scarcely time to bury one before the next became ill.

So I was sitting on the porch, inhaling the fresh air, when Dr. Redmond drove up in his borrowed car. He disembarked, tipped his hat to me, and sat down on the steps without invitation. His suit was wrinkled, his shirt stained, his hair mussed. I imagine I was in the same condition, and by that time, I didn't care. Vanity had departed my list of sensibilities.

"Miss Birdsong, I apologize for not stopping by sooner. I wanted to express my condolences on the loss of your brothers." He turned sideways, his back against the porch railing, and I could see the weariness in his eyes. "I would like to extend them to your mother as well."

I shook my head. "I hardly ever see her. She shows up for the funerals and then she's gone again. I fear we're about to have another." My eyes filled and I looked across the yard, where the grass was dying as well under the assault of frosty nights. "Micah is dying upstairs."

Dr. Redmond stood. "Would you like me to look at him? I don't know what I can—"

"Do? There's nothing anyone can do. It's out of our hands." I wiped my eyes with my apron. "It doesn't even seem to be in God's hands."

"We're all in God's hands, Miss Birdsong. We're always in God's hands, whether we're sick or well or dying or just walking down a lonely road."

A lonely road. That's where everything had begun to fall apart.

"You can placate yourself with that thought, Dr. Redmond, but I'm afraid I'm past all belief." I stood and tried to disguise my unsteadiness, but I'm certain he noticed. I imagine my previous reticence caused him not to comment.

I showed him to Micah's bedroom, where Thracia kept the deathwatch. Watching was her best talent, and she had put it to good use these last days. Dr. Redmond walked past her and placed his bag on the bedside table. Feeling Micah's pulse, he said it was weak.

I watched Micah's face, a face I no longer knew. The brother I loved, the brother who knew my soul, had already begun his departure. I did not believe that I would ever see him again. I fell across the bed. "If this is what it's come to, I pray that if there is a God somewhere he will let me die, too," I cried.

Dr. Redmond put his hands on my back. His touch set off something, something primal, something so fearful I thought my heart would come out through my skin. I crawled away from him until I fell off the other side of the bed. "Miss Birdsong, I . . ."

"Don't ever touch me again," I whispered through my tears.

"I'm sorry. I was merely trying to comfort you."

"There is no comfort for me. Everyone I have ever loved has abandoned me. I'm left with almost nothing here. So forgive me if I have no use for solace."

He sat in the chair across the room as our silence filled the spaces unoccupied by Micah's labored breathing. I pulled myself onto the edge of the bed and held Micah's hand. His eyes opened for a moment. For a split second I thought I saw something there, something alive, something hopeful. But his eyes fluttered closed again. They closed for the last time.

My last brother, the brother I loved best, was dead.

I lay my head on his chest, hoping that his heart would start beating again, that maybe in this world such a thing as a miracle could occur. Taking his wrists in my hands, I waited, hoping the pulse would return, hoping, not praying, hoping, hoping. But as time went on, Dr. Redmond came over and, at a safe distance, told me gently that I had to let him go.

I thought the last vestiges of my life died then. But I was to be proven wrong, and in a way I would not have suspected.

8

THE FIERY PIT

We stood about chest deep in the trough we had dug. I was covered in dirt, as was Mother.

The trough would hold the body of my last dead brother.

Mother and I were standing in Micah's grave.

The unending task of burying the town's dead had exhausted all the grave diggers. No household was untouched by the deadly contagion. No day passed without a funeral procession, although the numbers attending grew fewer as the population decreased. Dr. Redmond's admonitions against public gatherings went unheeded when it came to funerals, although most folks were too busy tending their own invalids to come, or had given up mourning altogether, leaving the dead to bury their own.

That's how I felt by then. Dead. My heart lay in my chest, beating as usual, but the spirit behind it lay fallow and dry, like the plants in Mother's garden that withered away during the sharp autumn nights. I looked at the row of newly covered graves that contained the remains of my family—Charley, Wilson, Teddy, Nehemiah, and Jeremiah—then into the void where Micah's body would soon lay. I refused to think of his spirit, his soul. I thought I had no hope of meeting him again, now that I was unsure of my faith in God and any expectation of an afterlife, of paradise, of heaven.

Leaning against the spade, I watched Mother dig the grave of her last dead son. When I could find no one else to dig it, I had searched the town until I found her. If I was to bear this last burden, I would not bear it alone, or with the maddeningly silent Thracia, who even now sat against a tree, eating an apple and watching us destroy what was left of our own health. Thracia's industriousness didn't extend to care of the dead.

Mother's face was expressionless. As each shovelful of dirt passed over the side, she made no sound, uttered no words. We had spoken little since Jeremiah's death. Of course, she was present for all the funerals and accepted the condolences of our neighbors and the townspeople, but I had the feeling her mind wasn't even on the premises. Her body had simply arrived and did what came naturally. Thank you for your concern. I appreciate your coming. Oh, doesn't that cake look delicious.

I leaned against the side of the grave—my dress was already filthy, so more dirt wouldn't matter—and propped my elbow on the edge. A dizzy feeling came over me. I breathed heavily, trying to let it pass.

"We don't have all day, child," Mother said, her movements rhythmic and smooth. "The minister will arrive soon to bury this poor boy."

"This poor boy is your son." I tried to catch her eye, but that type of contact had been lost as well.

She continued digging. "Every poor boy has a mother somewhere."

"This is not becoming to you, Mother. All your sons die in quick succession, and all you can do is talk about them as if they belonged to someone else."

"They do belong to someone else, child. They belong to the heavenly Father now. There is nothing more I can do."

I threw down the spade. "If you had stayed at home and tended to your own family, perhaps you could have done something. Out of all those tonics and remedies, surely you possessed some knowledge that could have saved your sons." My voice broke. "They were my brothers."

She stopped and wiped sweat from her forehead with the back of her hand. "Only the Lord saves," she said, motioning to Thracia to help her out. "I am merely the Father's instrument." Thracia came over and offered her free hand, continuing to eat the apple she held in the other. Once she had Mother out, I heaved the spade over the side, and Thracia pulled me out as well.

Just then three figures entered the cemetery gate: Mim, and Odessa and Pandora. I had not seen them in weeks, as they kept themselves secluded for fear of contracting the illness. I approached Mim, but she held up her hand.

"I came only to grieve the loss of my grandchildren. Word came that Micah had died. Are you showing any symptoms, Wren?" Mim pulled her shawl around her and folded her arms, peering into the uneven grave. Her stoic demeanor began to falter as her eyes took in the remaining graves, the mounds of soil covering the remains of her beloved grandsons.

"No, Mim. Just exhaustion. And exasperation." At this I heaved a sigh in Mother's direction.

121

Apparently sensing warfare, the sisters launched a spiritual from their arsenal:

Didn't you hear Heaven bells ringin'?
Yes, I heered Heaven bells ringin'.
Didn't you hear Heaven bells ringin'?
Yes, I heered Heaven bells ringin',
Heaven bells ringin' in my soul,
Heaven bells ringin' in my soul,
Not a bit of evil in my soul,
Not a bit of evil in my soul.

"For mercy's sake, the funeral hasn't begun yet," Mim admonished, pulling out a white kerchief and dabbing her eyes as the sisters piped down. Odessa pulled some snuff from her pocket, packed a wad between her cheek and gum, offered some to Pandora, who took it eagerly, then offered it to me. I shook my head. Enough was going wrong without my resorting to snuff dipping.

"Wren, what in the world has happened to you?"

I turned and saw Miss Lanie Lansdale approach, stylish and immaculate as ever. I brushed the dirt from my hands and accepted Miss Lanie's embrace stiffly, trying not to muss her beautiful outfit.

"There were no grave diggers . . ." I offered, self-conscious and trying to wipe the dirt from my dress, which was surely ruined by the day's work.

"My child, I don't wonder at it. I've had to close the school and send everyone home. Dr. Redmond suggested that I do so, and I thought his advice sage. I wonder that we all haven't caught it ourselves. I suppose it is only through the Lord's gracious mercy that we have been spared."

The Lord's gracious mercy. Where had that mercy been through all this loss and hurt and pain? Why had he abandoned us all and broken us apart? Why was he destroying our lives this way? Why had he destroyed mine?

I didn't answer Miss Lanie because other mourners were arriving, as was the hearse containing Micah's coffin, which Mother and I had pieced together with wood left over from the succession of coffins we had been forced to construct. It was not a pretty coffin, nor dignified, as Micah deserved. It wasn't a coffin fit for a dog, but it was all we had the strength left to build.

The minister came, and a couple of men who helped the undertaker unload the coffin. The undertaker left immediately.

"I wonder who else died today?" Mim asked, watching him leave in haste. "The town is filled with so much sorrow."

"Oh, Wren, I nearly forgot," Miss Lanie whispered to us both. "Sloan Lowe."

"What about Skeeter?" I felt my soul grow colder, and my back stiffened at the mention of his name.

"He died yesterday. Succumbed to this illness, like so many others."

At that, I felt my heart lift. Mind you, it wasn't as if my spirit soared. I was too far gone for that. Nevertheless, the news that Sloan "Skeeter" Lowe no longer walked the earth ranked as good news.

"When is his funeral?" I asked, careful not to betray my emotions.

"Why, right after your brother's. I thought perhaps you were planning to stay for that one. I thought surely you would want to pay your respects to his parents, despite your feelings for him."

Miss Lanie didn't know what Skeeter had done to me, and I did not wish her to know now. Skeeter's deed would die with him. I saw no need for anyone to know.

"I think I may," I replied. "It would be the civil thing to do."

I watched the men place Micah's coffin next to the grave. They, too, beat a hasty retreat. I guessed we women would have to lower the casket. Something else we had to bear. Women bear the children, bear the pain, bear the grief. Women bear the heartache and the solitude of being misunderstood and the affliction of loving men and sons and brothers and fathers who barely notice our existence, all the while expecting all our attention to be focused on theirs. When they die too young, or too soon, or in ways too horrible to comprehend, then we must bear the loss with a fortitude forged through tears, through endless nights, through sun-shot days when the light hurts our eyes, and through storms of piercing thunder and rain that reflect the storms of our hearts.

Our minister, Reverend Ford, kept the service brief and steady. His words barely registered in my wearied mind, and I would not have given them any heed if they had. I wasn't sure I had any use for the Bible, or Jesus, or comfort and peace.

I watched the service as if through a leaded window, until Mim stepped forward. She asked Reverend Ford for his Bible and opened it and read a passage I had heard before, from the prophet Ezekiel.

" 'All the fowls of heaven made their nests in his boughs, and under his branches did all the beasts of the field bring forth their young, and under his shadow dwelt all great nations,' " she read. " 'Thus was he fair in his greatness, in the length of his branches: for his root was by great waters.

" 'The cedars in the garden of God could not hide him: the fir trees were not like his boughs, and the chestnut trees were not like his branches; nor any tree in the garden of God was like unto him in his beauty. I have made him fair by the multitude of his branches: so that all the trees of Eden, that were in the garden of God, envied him.'"

She closed the Bible and ran her gloved hand across its cracked leather binding before handing it back to the minister. "Our family has lived long and deeply within the history of Rutledge County. Our roots were strong and deep, and we held the promise of growing a tree that would have spread its branches into the future." Walking along the row of graves, she shook her head, and I could see her eyes fill with tears. It was the first sign of humanity anyone had shown—a true and articulate and authentic grief over the overwhelming loss.

"We were the envy of the trees of Eden. Like the biblical nations, our family rose beyond our beginnings, but we were not to stand until the end." She came back, taking a few seconds at each grave, marked only with simple wooden crosses, each bearing the name of these cherished grandsons, and sons, and brothers. "Our family was like a nation unto itself." She looked up. "Oh, dear Lord, how are we to rise again? What did we do that we were struck down to this? Is this to be our judgment? The price for our pride?"

She brought her head down and looked at Mother. Then Mim seemed to forget her self-imposed isolation. She went to Mother and took her hands, although Mother couldn't seem to acknowledge her at all and just stood there while Mim continued her lament.

"I was wrong to stay away from you and Wren," she said, reaching out to me. Had I not been so weary and numb, perhaps her tears would have drawn out my own, but none came. "I wish it had been me instead," she whispered. "There's no use for this, no sense to it. No reason for all this loss and pain."

The time came to lower the coffin. Mother, Thracia, and I grabbed the ropes, as did Mim, who prodded the sisters to help as well. There we were—three generations of women, left to ourselves after years of nurturing generations of men who were expected to carry on the family name, the bloodlines, to become the new pillars of Bethel Creek. We lowered the coffin, lowered the last of those hopes with my brother's body, ashes to ashes, dust to dust. Mother and I filled the grave with the mound of dirt it had taken us all morning to create, as Mim cried the tears the rest of us could not summon.

When we finished, Miss Lanie placed a small bouquet of flowers on the mound and patted me on my filthy hand, taking away a streak of black earth on her immaculate white glove. "Dear Wren, I so wish you would come by the school someday soon. We can read poetry and drink Earl Grey tea and try to put all this sadness behind you." She kissed me on the cheek and left.

Tea and poetry. It was a pleasant thought. Once those things would have been important. Not anymore. I was afraid to speak alone with Miss Lanie, afraid that I would grow sentimental and tell her all that had happened and offend her civilized sensibilities. Surely she would not understand, could not fathom any such violence against a woman. Miss Lanie's was a world of fragile china, imported lace, and cultured conversation, and her world did not broach the vulgar aspects of *our* world, aspects to which I wished I had not been exposed. I did not wish to expose anyone to what had happened. Especially such a dear friend and mentor.

I went over to where the mourners were gathering for Skeeter's last rites, a much larger crowd than the one that had shown up for Micah. Mim stood with Skeeter's parents, but I kept my distance, lest I blurt out what a malevolent child of darkness their precious child had turned out to be. As I watched from the crowd's periphery, Skeeter's coffin was brought in by his equally cursed friends—I was now convinced that all male persons of my age were of the same ill intent and kept my distance—and placed next to the grave.

The Lowe family plot was in an appropriate area of the cemetery, a sunken stretch near the edge of the swamp bounding the property. The ground tended to bounce under the weight of so many people and featured small peat bogs that were home to the Venus flytrap. I remembered when my brothers were interested in entomological matters—studying things that fly rather than trying to fly themselves—and we would come down here and watch the plants as they ate their prey.

The minister proceeded to praise Skeeter far above his attributes, probably more to please Mrs. Lowe than anything else. Don't speak ill of the dead—Mim's words came into my mind, and it was *all* I wanted to do. I wanted to shout it, but propriety and the knowledge that I would then come under the town's scrutiny held me back. A rape victim was painted as guiltier than the perpetrator in those times. I was still mindful of that.

So he preached on as I stood there and seethed, wishing I could take my spade, open that coffin, and kill Skeeter myself, exact my own justice on this man who had taken so much from me. I wanted revenge. It seemed too easy that a mere illness had taken him, albeit a ghastly one that probably caused him a great deal of suffering.

The minister finished, and Skeeter's friends began to lower him into the grave when a mist of smoke enveloped them. A whisper passed through the crowd. The boys continued to lower the coffin as the cloud grew thicker.

A thin flame shot from the grave.

Everyone stood in disbelief, except me. Papa had brought me down here alone once, many years ago, and pointed out the peat bogs that dotted the landscape, much like the bogs on the Isle of Skye, one of our ancestral homelands. He explained how the bogs would sometimes catch fire and burn for days or months or sometimes even years. A careless toss of a lit match or dying cigarette ember could set one ablaze.

This crowd had a different explanation.

"He's going into the everlasting fire," someone hissed, and many in the crowd gasped.

The boys let go of the ropes. The coffin fell into the pit as the crowd began to walk, then run away from the cemetery. They jumped on their horses or climbed into their buggies or dove into their cars, and soon all were gone, save Mr. and Mrs. Lowe, who looked at each other, bewildered, wondering what had just happened.

I walked over to the grave and looked. A thin flame licked against the side of Skeeter's coffin. For a moment I wished that coffin would burn until my malefactor's body was truly ashes and dust.

I turned away from the grave. Perhaps now I could turn away from the past. With my brothers gone, the evil one who had destroyed a precious part of me gone, I thought I could use the remainder of this day to reflect upon my losses and look to my future, to how I could bring my life away from these tragedies and find a way to become something other than a glorified maid and cook, a substitute mother and father to a crowd of unruly boys, most of whom had never even bothered to tell me that they loved me.

Then a feeling struck me—a deep and biting remorse for all my vengeful thoughts against my brothers. For all my complaints, I had loved them all, together and apart from one another, for their quirks and foibles and strengths, which they each had in abundance. Children seldom express love to one another in words—I suppose I failed to tell them I loved them as well, and now the opportunity was lost. I reflected on the men they might have become—soldiers and adventurers and poets and dreamers—and wondered how long it would take for this terrible ache in my heart to disappear.

But as I walked away, a wave of nausea consumed me, and I ran behind one of the taller monuments, where I became ill. Skeeter's mother came over to see after me. Mother had departed earlier, off to see another patient, someone she was not related to by blood. Mim and the sisters had left as well.

"Wren, darling, are you all right?" Mrs. Lowe placed a hand on my forehead. "You're burning up." She raised her black veil over her hat and peered into my eyes. "We need to get you home."

"I'll be okay. It's just a touch of what's going around," I said, wiping my chin on my sleeve. The dress was already ruined; another stain wasn't going to make a difference. "Thracia will take me home." She had been standing in the shadows, my constant companion. At that point, I guess I could have told her to go away, but somehow I didn't have the heart.

When I straightened, a light-headed feeling came over me. I collapsed onto the ground. My ears felt as if they were full of cotton, and I couldn't see clearly.

It occurred to me that I might be next. That soon, Mother would have to dig my grave alone, bury me alone, mourn me alone; she would have no one left. Maybe then she would appreciate all that she had lost.

I became aware of a face, of a soft voice near my ear. Someone lifted me and put me into the surrey. Someone was driving me home, and it wasn't Thracia. It was a man in a suit, a black suit of clothes and a dark hat, and I thought that Death had surely stopped for me, as Miss Dickinson so eloquently described in her poems. I was beyond thinking about heaven, but death had become a familiar being.

Somewhere in the fog of my brain, I remembered another man's touch, and I began to scream and thrash until I felt a sharp pain in my arm.

I slept. I don't know for how long, but when I awoke I felt as if my entire body was on fire. Everything ached. The nausea that enveloped me was overwhelming. I felt hands touching my body. I fought against them until I realized that no matter how hard I fought, those hands would continue to wash me and press me back into the sheets and attempt to soothe my hysterics.

I heard them talking about influenza. I'm not sure who I heard—perhaps Mother, although I doubted she would have come home merely to save her daughter, perhaps Dr. Redmond, maybe Mim. I heard them talk of fever and chills.

There was something about an armistice. I didn't know what they were talking about. Something about the end of the war.

Someone kept saying something about a child. A baby. Someone said a baby was coming.

Something about this news seemed to comfort me. I loved babies. Sweet and innocent of the world's evils. God's consolation for the struggles of life is how I had always thought of them.

I wondered who was coming. I didn't know anyone who was expecting a child.

It would be another month before I recovered from the influenza.

Only then would I realize who was bringing a child into this shattered world. That the one having a baby was me.

9

LIFE EVERLASTING

Mother slouched in a chair across the room, glowering as if I had broken all ten commandments at once. I was weak and thirsty. My mind was still trying to grasp the fact that my body was carrying the child of a man who had done terrible things to me, the child of a man who was now dead.

I tried to rise up on my elbows, but my arms were too weak to hold my weight. I fell back against the pillows and rolled my head to the side. A tall glass of water sat on the bedside table, just out of my reach.

"Could you help me, Mother?" It was the first time I had asked anything of her in months. I thought it was a simple request.

She stood and walked slowly toward the table, where she stood for a moment staring at the glass. Picking it up, she took a long, slow drink before throwing the remainder on my face.

Water filled my nose and eyes. I rubbed the drops away and tried again to sit up. Mother pushed me back, her knee on the edge of the bed, her hands so firmly on my shoulders that pain seared through my exhausted body.

"I did not raise my daughter to be a slattern," she said, grabbing me and pulling me into an upright position. "I raised you on Christian principles, on the laws of our most gracious heavenly Father, and you humiliate me by lying with a man outside of marriage and getting yourself with child."

"I did not get myself with child," I whispered through clenched teeth, not just from pain but from righteous anger. "I did not go out and do this. You are wrongly accusing me."

"I knew those newfangled ideas of Miss Lanie Lansdale would bring you to no good end." She let me go and paced the room, wagging her finger in the air. "She is a woman who does not know her proper place—coming down here with her liberal Northern ideas and casting them upon callow minds. She destroyed your sense of morality, and now you have finished the job."

I managed to swing my legs over the edge of the bed. My head swam. I suddenly felt hungry, but no food was in sight, and Mother stood between me and the kitchen. Thracia didn't seem to be around. Why I thought of food then I don't know. Perhaps it was my body talking. My mind was certainly unprepared for the verbal assault Huldah Birdsong had decided to unleash.

"Who is the father of this child?" Mother's face loomed in front of mine. Her hair was coming unpinned, and through my blurry eyes she appeared a Medusa whose snaked hair threatened to envelop my head with its ominous extrusion. "He must do right by you. He must marry you and give this child his name." She began shaking me by the shoulders again. "Tell me his name!"

I tried to fight her off, but I was too weak. I began to cry. "It won't make any difference," I said, slowly, quietly. "He's gone."

"Gone? You mean he's left town? Was he someone from the train? Someone who left for the war? Are you going to tell me, child? Are you going to tell me who it is?"

"He's dead, Mother." My voice returned, strong and defiant. "And I would not have married him had he lived."

"You are telling me that you would defy convention, defy the sanctified laws of God and lie to me and bring a child into this world, a woman alone, and allow everyone in this town whose respect I have worked so long and hard to obtain to speak ill of you and treat you as a pariah?"

I bit my lip and stared out the window, feeling her breath against my face.

"You would dishonor your father and me this way?"

"I was the one who was dishonored." I refused to meet her eyes.

Mother backed away. "I don't know what to make of that. You entice some boy into impure acts and then have the gall to say you were the one dishonored."

"Skeeter Lowe forced himself on me." I could scarcely hear my own voice. I felt small in body and spirit. Mother lunged at me.

"How dare you speak ill of the dead! I would dare you to say those things to Mrs. Lowe."

"Since when did you become Mim's sycophant?"

Mother recoiled. Like the day in the milliner's, she got a strange look in her eye that made me fear perhaps that if the influenza didn't kill me, nor humiliation, she would surely strangle me herself. She went back across the room and sat down, putting her head in her hands.

I watched her for several moments as she wept. Offering comfort or sympathy to someone who is intent on condemning you for sins you have not even thought of committing is difficult. Then I guess I felt as cold toward my own mother as I felt toward anything else that had happened. I realized that even the house was cold—no one had thought to stoke the fire. It had burned down to embers and smoke, which swirled into the chimney to disappear into the sky, the place where my brothers longed to live, the place where I now wished I could join them.

"You say he forced himself on you?" Mother's voice startled me, and I finally looked her in the face.

"Did you stop to wonder why Thracia has been here with me since the day Charley died?"

"You mean the day Charley went away." She said it abruptly. I had forgotten in my influenza-induced haze that *died* was a forbidden word, much as it was forbidden to say that Papa had left us.

I sighed. "Yes." I lay back down. "Thracia probably kept Skeeter from killing me. It's a wonder she didn't kill him, the way she hit him on the head with that rock."

"Hit him on the head." Mother stood straight and walked to the window. "No. It couldn't have been . . ."

"Couldn't have been what?"

"Skeeter had a large lump on his head. Mrs. Lowe asked me to look at it."

"When was this?" I couldn't believe Mother had gone to see after Skeeter when I was left to tend my own dying brothers.

"A couple of days after Charley left this last time. Skeeter was having trouble seeing. Double vision."

135

A diagnosis of double vision from a woman who was blind to what had happened to her own flesh and blood. I could see Mother putting together the events.

"You came home," she said, her head tilted to one side. "Your dress was dirty and torn—and you were soaked with the rain that fell that afternoon." She raised her hands to her cheeks and closed her eyes. "Dear heavenly Father, I am blind, deaf, and dumb."

I agreed with the words of her prayer but did not echo it.

She came to me then, looked into my eyes, and placed her hand on my belly. "The boy left you with child."

I closed my eyes and felt the tears trickle into my hair.

In a moment, I heard Mother leave the room, closing the door quietly behind her. I opened my eyes and listened, but all I could hear was the silence of the house, that crushing silence I thought I would someday enjoy. Only I could never have imagined the way it came about. Or that anything could ever change it now.

> I had a little bird
> And its name was Enza.
> I opened the window
> And in-flew-Enza.

The little ditty ran over and over in my head. I had overheard some little girls singing it the last time I was in Bethel Creek. They were jumping rope to the tune, apparently oblivious to its meaning.

I wasn't sure why it began running through my head. Perhaps it was to fill the space put there by the overwhelming silence of the house.

Our house had always been a maelstrom of activity, filled with the shouts and exclamations of six raucous boys who passed through like a cross between an inferno and a cyclone. The air in the house swirled with the currents they produced, and their voices flowed through the rooms regardless of walls or closed doors.

Now that Mother and Thracia and I were the only occupants, the sounds of the house itself took over. There was the occasional interruption—the clang of a pot in the kitchen, the rustle of a newspaper, the slap of the screen door—but for the most part, the house filled the void. Creaks I had never before noticed woke me in the night, and sounds like boards splitting apart rent the air at odd moments. Sometimes I thought I heard the sound of a door close, when I knew no one was coming or going.

The house remembered, is what it was. The building knew the boys were gone, but it kept on producing the sounds they made as they trammeled their way through it each day. The house knew what sound to produce at what time and kept its duty diligently, startling me and Mother, too, although she would hardly admit that she found the continued reminders disconcerting.

I took to thinking about anything to drown out the noise. I played our Victrola until I nearly wore out the cylinders. I played the piano badly, until Mother screamed at me to stop. One day I walked up to Thracia and dared her to speak. She looked back, her eyes blank, and I wanted to snatch every one of those long black hairs from her head.

The problem was that no one cried, and no one dared do it. It would be like admitting they were all really gone—Papa, Charley, Teddy, Wilson, Micah, Nehemiah, Jeremiah. Seven souls missing from our home, which was now occupied by three silent women who didn't know how to grieve such a loss.

Then something began to change.

As the autumn wore on and the nights grew cold, I realized that the child I carried had begun to grow.

Mother had stated that it was a miracle I hadn't lost the child during my sickness. She fully expected that the child would not come to term, given the burden placed on my body.

Then one day as I sat on the porch rocking, trying to find some solace in an Indian summer day, I went to smooth my skirt and realized my body felt different. Rounder. Fuller.

I put my hands on my belly to be sure of what I was feeling. It wasn't a drastic change—I didn't really even show yet. It was too soon.

The child was alive.

My child was alive.

I refused to think of it as Skeeter's child. If I did, it would become a child of malevolence, and I would not allow that. This child must be mine and mine alone. I would be its only parent. I would raise it and love it—I did remember what that was, in spite of everything. Love transcended unbelief in my mind and could still exist for me, but only on grounds that I chose.

I wondered how long it would be before I would feel the baby move. When I became aware that my child had begun to grow within my body, I felt a joy I had not felt in months. I wanted to share it with someone.

As with the violation itself, Miss Lanie would have been the obvious choice. However, she still didn't know what had happened to me. I had avoided her since the day I learned I was carrying a child, because I knew that in time it would become evident.

So, like Micah, I had become a prisoner of my own home. I didn't go to church—the epidemic had relented and the churches were open again, but between my dormant faith and fear of further humiliation, I couldn't bring myself to go—or to buy supplies. I sent Thracia, or Mother went in my stead if nothing else could be done. Mim and the sisters came around from time to time, but they were nowhere to be seen that day.

I decided to take a chance on telling Mother. She had gone out into her garden earlier that day and hadn't even bothered coming inside for dinner. I walked around the house and through the gate.

First, our nation had gone to war in foreign lands. Then we fought a war on our own soil against an unseen foe that took lives and destroyed families without mercy.

Now Huldah Birdsong was waging war against herself.

Evidence of carnage lay everywhere. She had chopped trees to nubs, their stumps ravaged by the ax. Dead plant stalks were scattered across the plot; they were already dry from the chilly nights, so it had probably been little effort to finish them off. All that was already dead had been pulled up by the roots; all that was still living suffered an early demise.

Mother scrounged across the ground on her hands and knees. She had destroyed every bit of vegetation in that square of earth.

I walked among the ruins, pausing here and there to study the plants, to discern what I might salvage. For some reason, I felt a sudden rush of affection for that garden—it seemed like all we had left of our past life—and now Mother seemed intent on destroying it as well.

Mother looked up for a second, blinking her eyes against the sun, looking at me as if she didn't even recognize me. I forgot for a moment why I had come to find her.

"What are you doing?" I sank to my knees beside her. Ordinarily, I would have felt angry with this display. Now

I felt confused and frightened. She was the only person I had left to turn to, and the fear that she might come after me next was more than I could take.

"It's all wrong," she said, her voice quivering as if from cold, although I could see the perspiration soaking through her dress. "This is a garden to the glory of God, and none of it is right."

"I don't understand what you mean."

She waved her hands over the ground. "I cannot have a proper biblical garden without a tree of life."

I blinked. "I didn't know there was such a thing. I thought that was something found only in the Garden of Eden."

"The good Lord put it here as part of creation, so it must exist somewhere in the world. These are ignoble complements for such a divine creation."

What had formerly been a stand of life everlasting lay in front of me, the dried white flowers strewn across the ground. Odessa and Pandora had told Mother of a tea she could make from it, one that would stave off the rages of the influenza.

But Mother had ignored them. Although her repertoire of remedies included teas made from practically everything else on the place, if Odessa and Pandora suggested something, Mother was sure to ignore it, thinking it voodoo or something to do with some African curse. In the throes of my illness, I would have drunk anything short of poison to gain relief from the cough that ravaged my lungs to the point where I believe I cracked some ribs. My body was still sore.

Now even life everlasting was no match for Huldah Birdsong.

Mother was intent on her work. I didn't know how else to get her attention, so I just blurted it out.

"The baby's growing."

She kept pulling up plants.

"I said, the baby's growing. I can feel myself getting bigger."

"I heard you the first time."

"That means the baby's going to live, doesn't it?"

"Yes, probably so." She pushed a strand of hair from her face and surveyed the devastation. "We need to plow all this up while you can still work."

"That's all you can think of to say to me?" I stood and dusted off my skirt. Mother stood as well but didn't bother dusting off anything.

"It's a child. I had seven. Now I have one. Some live, some die. Some die before they're born. Some die right after. Some just go away, and mothers never see them again. Better that it die in the womb than live in this vale of tears."

I wanted to slap her, but I had already seen where that led. I couldn't believe what she said next.

"You need to start thinking about who you're going to give it to." She walked calmly to the fence, where she picked up a rake and began furiously raking the refuse into small piles, then together into one large one.

"What do you mean, who I'm going to give 'it' to? This is not an 'it'; this is a baby, and the baby's not someone else's. This baby's mine."

"Well, you cannot keep *this baby*. Everyone will assuredly know then that you are a fallen woman."

"I am not a fallen woman. This was done to me. I can't help that, but this child is mine and mine alone. I won't let you or anyone else take it away from me."

She took a box of matches from her apron pocket, struck one against the fence, and tossed it onto the pile, which became a bonfire in seconds. The heat seared my face, and I backed away.

Mother took her rake and went out through the gate.

"Then you best prepare to suffer the consequences of that decision," she called over her shoulder. "And be prepared to leave once the child comes."

"Leave?" I followed her to the house.

"I'm not raising your child."

"But this would be your grandchild."

"It is a child of sin. I will not have it under my or your father's roof."

He's not here anymore! I wanted to scream. I looked at her back as she walked away.

"You stay back there and mind that fire. Don't let it get into the house or the barn." The screen door slapped behind her.

I noticed Thracia swinging back and forth in the tree swing that hung from an old oak in the backyard. She had apparently finished the wash, and neither my mother or I had noticed that she had hung it out as we fought a battle of our own.

"Did you hear that?" I paced the yard as Mother's Garden of Eden burned to ashes. "I can't help it how I came by this child." I stopped and pressed my hands to my eyes, then to my belly. "Skeeter was the one who sinned, not me!" I shouted, hoping Mother would hear. "I'm the one sinned against."

"I'm not going anywhere," I told Thracia, who swung back and forth, back and forth, until I couldn't watch anymore.

"You hear that!" I shouted at the house. "I'm not going anywhere! I'm keeping my baby!" I stumbled back to the fire and stared into the dying flames. "No one is making me give my child away," I whispered. "This baby is all that I have left. No one's making me give away my baby. Not even you, Mother. Especially not you."

142

10

GOOD NEWS
FROM A FAR COUNTRY

December grew as frigid as the silence that expanded between Mother and me. I could not reason with her. She was adamant that I give up the child as soon as it was born, that neither she nor I brook any attachment to it. She spoke of families who would adopt babies, of orphanages, thoughts that nearly drove me out of what remained of my mind. I couldn't think of giving my child away to strangers when it had a mother ready to love and care for it, even if she had to do it in a shack in the woods.

I would have prayed for a miracle, but I no longer believed in prayer or miracles. Prayer had not stopped the evil that had brought me to this place, nor had a miracle saved the lives of my brothers or brought my father home.

In my philosophy, they did not exist. I call it philosophy, because that is what I had developed in place of faith.

The epidemic had subsided. Funerals came fewer and farther between. Mother was no longer called out to help the sick, partly because the epidemic was followed by an unprecedented wave of good health among the citizens of Bethel Creek. It was also because Dr. Connell Redmond had decided to stay on and open a medical practice in town.

I could tell this annoyed Mother no end. She had enjoyed her position as the town's acting physician, which was now usurped by one of the properly schooled variety. I knew her well enough to know what she must have been thinking: *It should be me. If only Mother had allowed me to go to medical school.* She was seething about it; that was obvious. Moreover, she had an unmarried pregnant daughter *and* a maddeningly silent Indian girl underfoot, one who had no proper reason for living with us other than we didn't have the heart to make her leave. Thracia provided a buffer between us at times, probably keeping us from hurling pots of boiling cabbage at one another or dousing each other with the wash water. Overall, I'm sure Mother was fit to be tied.

So our days went like this: We rose early in the morning. Mother had hired help to keep the farms running—they were our primary sources of income. We couldn't let the deaths of my brothers lead us all into privation, not when so many generations had fought and sweated over these parcels to make them fertile and prosperous. She would give the new workers instructions for the day. Then we sat down to breakfast, cooked by Thracia.

Thracia had taken over the room occupied by Charley, Teddy, and Wilson. I would not allow her into Micah's room. Although he had shared it with the two youngest, I still thought of it as his alone. I sat there many afternoons, reading his books and magazines, touching the pages his hands had touched, wishing I could hear his voice reading to me again. I allowed no one to disturb his things, not even Mother, and for once she respected my wishes. Of course, in her mind, no one was dead—they had just gone away for a little while.

Thracia was a superb cook. I regained the weight I had lost during my illness and began to grow round and not just with child. Thracia spiced her recipes in a way that made your mouth develop a mind of its own, devouring each luscious morsel so that even Tiberius and Titania began to complain when no scraps came their way at the end of a meal. I began preparing them a special portion, just to quash their insistent mewing. I couldn't figure out how Thracia came by her talent; I only knew that I was grateful for it every day.

We washed the clothes and bedding together, the only sounds the splash of water into the giant galvanized tubs and the swishing of fabric against washboards. When we hung the laundry on the long clotheslines, I pretended I was a child again, raising my arms and pushing against the drying sheets as they billowed and collapsed with the rise and fall of the wind. I encouraged Thracia to join me, and eventually she did. Once I almost saw her smile. It turned out there was someone in there after all. I just had to find a way to get her to come out.

Then Thracia would cook lunch, and we would devour everything again. During the afternoons, Mother either went to check on the few patients she had left to her, the ones who didn't trust "city doctors," or she spent hours reading her horticultural books, searching for that elusive tree of life that she had to have as her centerpiece in the new Garden of Eden.

145

As for myself, I wandered around the place, picking up pecans or grooming the horses. Mother wouldn't allow me to ride; she insisted the jostling would be bad for the baby. "We want it to be healthy for its new parents," she would proclaim. I fumed whenever she said this and refused to think of that day. This baby was going nowhere, but she would find that out when the time came.

And, like I said, I read. In my mind, I traveled to all the places I hoped to visit someday for real: the Orient, where I would explore Buddhist temples and drink tea in China. Northern Africa, where I would climb the pyramids of Egypt and ride a camel across the Sahara. I would paddle a canoe down the Amazon, scale the Alpine peaks, purchase the world's most divine clothing in the shops of Paris. I would do all this with my child at my side. Bethel Creek would not be this child's only experience of life. My child would live life in all its wide experience and glory, just as I now lived a life of unbounded fantasy because the real had become so disappointing that I had to have some means of escape.

Then something happened that made me believe deliverance was possible. We were saved from ourselves by an unexpected but welcome visitor.

Uncle Frederick McRae, Mother's brother, arrived on a bright, crisp morning a week before Christmas. He had *driven* all the way from San Francisco, California. Well, maybe not all the way. Still, he may as well have come from the moon, given the reception accorded him.

Micah and I had read volumes about that part of our country that seemed more like an exotic foreign outpost than a piece of our own great United States. How Uncle Frederick came to live there was a story of its own.

I only knew him from a photograph taken of Mother's entire family when they were much younger. Frederick had been a teenager, probably about my own age, and he had been very handsome, tall and sandy haired with a devilish grin. According to Mother, he had always had a reckless streak. He raced horses in Camden, where people came from all over the East Coast to see who owned the finest competitors. So it was no surprise that he signed up for the cavalry when the Spanish-American War broke out in 1898. He went to the Philippines, where he saw action and was injured for all his bravado.

Upon returning to the United States, he disembarked in San Francisco, which held many attractions for a man with his wide-ranging interests. He became a cosmopolitan and had not returned to South Carolina. Mother rarely even heard from him. Until now.

She barely recognized him. We were eating breakfast, a fine meal of fresh pork sausage—it was slaughtering season—fried ham, grits, biscuits slathered with butter and honey, hot applesauce, and strong, black coffee that could have lifted the table legs from the floor. A loud honking sound came from in front of the house. We all looked at each other before Mother finally rose to see who it was.

I followed her onto the porch. A man stood in the front yard next to an automobile that looked as if it had been driven through every type of weather that existed, from hailstorms to possibly even a tornado, because a large dent split the roof. It appeared to have been driven through oceans, lakes, deserts, and mountains—possibly even quicksand.

Mother squinted. "Sir, I do not recognize you. Have you come for medical assistance?" She put her hands on her hips as if daring the man to say yes.

The man took off his hat, smiled into the distance, then came around the car and up the steps. Striding up to

Mother, he looked her square in the face, then kissed her soundly on both cheeks, in the European style.

Mother stepped back, aghast, raising her hand to slap the stranger before recognition came. This was her long-lost brother.

She slapped him anyway, a light pop, and she laughed when she did it. It was the first time I had heard her laugh in anything like true amusement in months.

"That's some greeting," said Uncle Frederick, rubbing his cheek.

"That's for not letting a body know you were coming and for not coming home for years on end or letting us know whether you were alive or dead."

"Now how could I let you know I was alive if I was dead?" he said, smiling at me.

Of all the times Mother wants to know if someone is truly alive or dead! I couldn't believe what I was hearing.

"Frederick, you may not remember . . ."

"Wren. Mim wrote me that she had grown into a beautiful young lady and that she was trying desperately to marry her off to some local boy, someone she deemed an appropriate match."

I froze, as did Mother for a second. "That arrangement was purely a figment of Mim's imagination," Mother replied, to my surprise. "He was completely unsuitable for Wren."

Uncle Frederick took my hand, bowed, and kissed it. I drew my hand back quickly, sure he saw the fright on my face. Mother came to me.

"Don't mind her. She's a little skittish about people touching her since all of this influenza contagion."

He nodded. "It has decimated the country. All along the way, I encountered towns where funerals outnumbered births and wakes outnumbered weddings." He took Mother's hands in his. "Mim telegraphed me about the boys, Huldah. I am deeply sorry. Has Mallon come home?"

I waited to see how Mother would respond to this. She bit her lip. "I see Mim has been busy," she said, avoiding the question. "Well, as Proverbs says, 'As cold waters to a thirsty soul, so is good news from a far country.' You're the best news we've had in a while. Come in. We were just eating breakfast."

We went in to the laden table. Uncle Frederick rubbed his stomach and eased into a chair. "I haven't seen a table with this much food on it since I went away to war. Are you sure there's no man around to help eat it?"

"There is now," I said, getting another plate and some silverware. Thracia had remained inside and continued to eat, watching Uncle Frederick, who folded his hands under his chin and stared back.

"Who are you?"

"You might as well speak to the walls," Mother said. "Her name is Thracia. She does not honor us with her voice, only her presence."

My uncle shrugged and filled his plate.

"Did you drive all the way from California?" Mother asked, watching him cover his plate with a double layer of everything.

He laughed. "That was the original plan. It seems that I was overly optimistic."

"How so?" I asked before continuing to devour the contents of my own plate. My appetite grew daily, and I ate more like a twenty-five-year-old lumberman than a seventeen-year-old girl.

"It seems the highways of our great country are not suited for long-range travel. I have been up to my axles in mud more times than I can count. I may as well have come in a canoe in some spots. Lewis and Clark probably fared better." He paused a few moments to chew. "I guess you could say I slid more than I drove until finally I got wise and just put the car and myself on a train. Whenever I got to a stop, I would get my car, drive around the town, see the sights, then put the car back on the train and move on to the next stop. And so on, and so on." He stopped talking then and launched into the biscuits and sausage like a man in love with a devastatingly beautiful woman.

I started to ask him some more questions, but Mother motioned for me to remain silent, so Mother, Thracia, and I just sat there, watching this man eat his fill twice over. We refilled his coffee cup when it emptied and brought more butter when the dish ran out. Watching him sate himself satisfied a hunger I don't believe any of us knew we had. A hunger for someone else in our house, someone to break all that silence, someone to bring a new perspective to our limited lives.

I don't think any of us were aware of it until then. We could cope with the things we needed to do each day. We didn't *need* a man around the house. Yet what we all seemed to realize, I could feel it, was that we *wanted* a man around the house.

The tears came before I could stop them. I wanted my father to come home. I wanted my brothers alive again, tearing around the house, creating havoc. I missed having them to gripe about, because boys can always give a girl something to gripe about. Who would know that you could miss complaining about someone?

Uncle Frederick put down his fork and slid his hand across the table to mine. This time I didn't flinch. This was my uncle. He was family, and he was filling a place that badly needed filling.

"You must miss your brothers," he said, as if reading my mind, and patted my hand.

I nodded and dried my face with my apron. "Grief blind-sides me at odd moments. I apologize. This can't be much of a homecoming, when your own niece is crying at the breakfast table."

He kissed my hand again. "Family is for your best sides and your worst sides. Family are the only ones who truly understand."

It was a kind moment, and what I needed was kindness. It was something Mother was incapable of giving, and I wondered how two children from the same parents could have turned out so different.

Mother rapped her knuckles against the table, startling us both.

"Why, it's almost Christmas!" she said, suddenly in a bright mood. Uncle Frederick and I looked at each other, and I thought I detected the slightest sparkle in his eyes. "We must have a celebration!"

"A celebration?" I threw down my napkin. "After everything we've been through?"

"Of course. We are alive. We must celebrate the living. That's what Christmas is about, the celebration of new life through our Lord, Jesus Christ."

Your Lord, I thought. Although, perhaps I could get a little excited about a tree. I always enjoyed trimming the tree with the old decorations we brought down from the attic each year.

"I agree with you, Huldah," said my uncle. "We need a fine McRae family Christmas celebration."

With that, he pushed away from the table. It was only then that I realized something. He had been sitting in Papa's chair, and Mother hadn't said a word.

Perhaps Uncle Frederick's arrival signaled a new beginning.

Aromas filled our home on Christmas morning. The scent of a newly cut pine permeated the front room. Ham baked. Sweet potatoes boiled. Bayberry candles stood on the table, which was set with Mother's wedding china, china she had always deemed too fragile to use when the boys were alive. For a few days, we were transformed. We cleaned and cooked and rearranged. Uncle Frederick had gone into the woods on Christmas Eve morning and emerged with the most beautiful pine, amazingly symmetrical and perfect for our celebration. After placing it in the stand, he, Mother, and I spent the rest of the morning decorating the tree with fragile glass ornaments from Germany and strings of silver tinsel that glimmered in the light. The shape of the tree did not lend itself to candles, so we made do with speckled reflections of light on the walls, opening the draperies to the full power of the winter sun.

The rest of that day and the next morning, Mother and I went into a tizzy. Mother had sent out invitations via Thracia, whom we instructed to knock and present the envelopes, which would not require speaking, and wait for an R.S.V.P. from each person invited. The guest list was surprising in its breadth and generosity. Mim and the sisters were invited. Mother invited Miss Lanie, and Mrs. Lapis Cochrane, whose husband had succumbed to the influenza, and even Dr. Connell Redmond. Six guests and Uncle Frederick. Enough to fill the empty places at our table and then some. Everyone agreed to the invitation.

Except Thracia. As we decorated the tree, we realized someone was missing.

"Disappeared just as suddenly as she appeared," Mother huffed, draping tinsel over a branch.

"Perhaps she went to see family," said Uncle Frederick, struggling to put the topper on the tree.

"I don't believe she has any," I said, arranging pine and holly branches on the mantel.

"Everyone has family somewhere," he replied. "It's a matter of whether we own up to them or not."

I said, "Well, I've never seen her with anyone that resembles family."

So we dropped the matter and turned our attention to cooking.

Mother made a Japanese cake, the likes of which I had never seen anywhere else. She baked two layers of yellow cake and two chocolate layers with raisins. Then she made a lemon filling, which she placed between the layers and sprinkled with fresh coconut we had forced Uncle Frederick into shredding for us.

In fact, we found so many things for Uncle Frederick to do that he threatened to go back to San Francisco where he could get some rest. Besides busting open coconuts, he shelled pecans and walnuts, roasted chestnuts, and boiled a vat of peanuts over an open fire in the backyard. He groomed the horses—Saturn, Neptune, and my beloved Pegasus—then took them out and rode them hard over the crackly fields. The horses seemed to appreciate their liberation from the paddock and came back giddy from speed and freedom. How do you explain to an animal that its owner has died? The horses had felt the void, too, and no one had noticed.

By the time our guests arrived that bright, crisp Christmas noon, we had transformed our home from a house of mourning to a house of celebration. I began to feel some hope myself as I fingered the carved crèche and studied the mother Mary's expression as she adored her child—the Christ child.

Could it really have happened, that this woman of Nazareth, this woman lost to time, was chosen to bear the soul that would bring salvation to the world? I used to ponder how God could choose one person to do the one thing that would make so much difference to the whole of humanity throughout time. Of course, that was before I began to have doubts.

I now wondered how that same God who chose a woman to give virgin birth could allow another to bear a child of violence.

But I had to push those thoughts away. It was Christmas morning, 1918. Most of my family had died, but I was among the living, and our friends and neighbors were arriving for a feast.

Miss Lanie arrived in the company of Dr. Redmond, which was a surprise within itself. I remembered Mother's wish that Miss Lanie meet a handsome young doctor to tame her wild impulses. Perhaps this development would assuage Mother's budding rivalry with the good doctor.

Mrs. Cochrane came next, followed by Mim, Odessa, and Pandora, who struggled up the steps. Mim kissed me and hugged Uncle Frederick and Mother before casting aspersions on our glorious tree.

"I would think you would have dispensed with such foolishness after so much loss," she said to Mother, who was straightening tinsel that had flown off in the breeze created by the opening and closing door.

"It is the birthday of our Savior," Mother replied sharply, turning to face Mim. "We must celebrate his birth and Frederick's return. So if you believe this is foolishness, then why did you bother coming?"

Mim blinked. "I . . ."

"I see," Mother said, and she led us into the dining room.

We only used the dining room at Christmas and Thanksgiving, and for birthdays. I had polished the mahogany surfaces of the table and china cabinet until they gleamed. Then Mother had brought out a cream damask tablecloth that she saved only for the most special occasions and spread it across the table, which we had set with her fine china, silver, and crystal. The room sparkled like sun-kissed snow. As we served the dishes one by one, everyone exclaimed how wonderful everything looked, and I could tell Mother was pleased that our efforts were well appreciated.

Mother bowed her head to give thanks, and everyone followed suit, including me. I had neglected to tell her that I was really celebrating Christmas in the secular sense, but I bowed out of respect to her to avoid another conflagration.

"Heavenly Father, we give thanks to thee this most glorious day, this Christmas Day, for thy most divine gift of our Lord, Jesus Christ, who was born of humble beginnings and became the King for all time through his suffering for our most egregious sins and faults. We ask thee, Father, to give us all the spirit of Christ in our hearts, to give us hearts full of faith, hope, and charity that we might prove the sacrifice of Christ in our lives, and serve our fellow man as we serve thee. On this glorious Christmas Day, Father, we ask thy many blessings. In Jesus' name, Amen."

Everyone echoed the closing except me, and Mim shot me a look I won't soon forget. I think she may have been the first to suspect my defection from the faith, but this was Christmas, and even Mim knew better than to test the limits further, especially where Mother was concerned.

Miss Lanie took delicate bites of the corn-bread dressing. "I honestly believe that I have never tasted anything so delectable up North," she said, after chewing and wiping her mouth with the cloth napkins that matched the tablecloth.

"Nor in the West," Uncle Frederick replied, eating less delicately. In his case, I think you would more accurately describe it as shoveling, something at which my brothers had excelled.

Dr. Redmond looked at the green mass that covered a wedge of his plate. "If you will pardon my ignorance, what is this called?" He asked no one in particular. We all looked at each other before bursting into laughter.

"Have you never seen mustard greens?" Mother asked.

"You mean mustard, like the condiment?"

Mother shook her head. "You have come from another place. This is old-fashioned Southern cooking."

"That be's colored cooking," said Pandora, with Odessa nodding in agreement.

"Like slavery times," Odessa said, much to everyone's discomfiture, as she poked a hole in her biscuit with her finger, then filled the cavity with cane syrup. Slavery was a word never spoken, and Miss Lanie rushed to fill the conversational gap that ensued.

"Mr. McRae . . ."

"Please, lovely lady, call me Frederick."

It was the first time I had ever seen Miss Lanie blush.

"Frederick." She began again. "I wonder if you might tell us about San Francisco. I have traveled much but have never made it to our western states."

I had a small bowl of ambrosia, a simple mixture of fresh oranges mixed with grated coconut and sugar, which I devoured like it had come from Greece itself. As I savored the combination of sweet and tart, then attacked my heaping plate, Uncle Frederick regaled us with tales of the place he now considered his home.

"Where do I begin?" he said, looking wistful, as if his mind were traveling across the clouds to this place he loved so dearly that his birthplace now held little to pull him back.

"Describe it," Miss Lanie replied, taking another slice of steaming ham, sounding much like the schoolteacher that she truly was. "The land, the people, the buildings."

Everyone at the table leaned forward with interest. Even Mrs. Cochrane, who hadn't said a word since arriving, looked as if she were as hungry for a good story as she was for the dressing she was quickly putting away.

"Living in San Francisco is like living at the world's busiest crossroad. It teems with people from all over the world, going from here to there, with dreams and aspirations that float around them like the fog that envelops us all each morning."

"I ain't like no fog," Odessa said. "Can't see nothing coming nor going. Fog be a place where's animals and manimals hide."

Uncle Frederick laughed while Mim shot the sisters a sideways look. In prior years, Mother would have relegated them to the kitchen for their meal. In deference to their age, she decided they deserved a space at the table as much as any of us. Even Tiberius and Titania stood sentry on opposite sides of the table, in case some choice morsel should find its way to the floor.

"Are cable cars still the preferred form of transportation there?" Dr. Redmond asked in a more practical vein.

"Given the hills and valleys of our landscape, they are the most effective means of traversing the city." Uncle Frederick paused for a few moments to down some dressing and turnips. "The city is full of Chinamen and Russians and Spaniards. The sounds of exotic languages fill the streets."

157

"I suppose it is even more diverse since the opening of the canal," Dr. Redmond added, referring to the Panama Canal, which had opened only a few years earlier.

"The city has burgeoned. The docks are full not only with fishing boats but with ocean liners full of voyagers and freighters carrying goods around this vast world of ours."

"I thought the earthquake in 1909 destroyed much of the city," Miss Lanie said.

"The year was 1906, my dear lady." I couldn't believe it; she blushed again. "Much of the city *was* destroyed, but it has since been rebuilt, and in a grand style."

"I remember the shake," Pandora said.

"'The shake'?" Dr. Redmond looked at her, confused.

"She means the Charleston earthquake, back in 1886," Mim said. "That's what the colored folks call it, the shake."

"The land was shakin' in Bethel Creek, too," Odessa said, defending her sister. Mim rolled her eyes. "The crick even flowed backwards."

Mim sighed with impatience. "Now you're just telling stories. Hush up and let Frederick tell his." She spread some homemade chowchow pickle on her potato salad. "Now, son, I want you to tell me more about what you do out there. How do you make your living? You've never quite made that clear."

Uncle Frederick cleared his throat. "I'm in the import business."

"What do you import?" Dr. Redmond asked, picking at his mustard greens as if they were about to go crawling across the table.

"Commodities from the Orient," he said, avoiding everyone's eyes and concentrating again on shoveling food into his mouth.

Mother squinted at him. "That tells us nothing."

"Knickknacks, bric-a-brac. Jade Buddhas, Chinese porcelain dogs, perhaps a few gewgaws of the human variety." The corners of his mouth twitched.

Miss Lanie leaned forward, her eyes gleaming. Why is there something about a rogue that always catches the female's attention, no matter how highly cultured or refined she thinks herself?

I had asked Uncle Frederick about this the day before. He explained that sometimes people couldn't afford passage to America. Consequently he greased a few palms so those intrepid souls could ride along with the cargo. Although it was hazardous in many ways, my uncle saw it as a public service. "I consider it part of my mission in life," he had explained. "People who had the courage to leave their homes and travel into the unknown built this country. Why shouldn't I help make our country stronger?"

Mother stood, placing her hands flat on either side of her plate.

"Are you importing prostitutes?"

Miss Lanie gasped. Dr. Redmond hid a smile behind his napkin. Mim was not amused. I dropped my fork, which clattered against the china plate and startled the sisters, who yelled "Have mercy!" in unison.

"Daughter, I will not have you accusing my son of promulgating ill-gotten gains," Mim said, standing, too.

"Well, I will not sit by and have a purveyor of the carnal arts eat at my table as if he taught Bible class at Sunday school. I am quite well-read. I know what goes on in these big cities. New York, Philadelphia, Chicago, San Francisco—they're all the same. They've gotten away from the Word of God. Lot's wife wouldn't even have to turn around to be turned into salt, what with all that goes on." She stomped around the table, then stopped behind

Frederick's chair. "I know. I'll get Mallon. He will sort this out for us." With that, she marched into the backyard and we could hear her calling my father's name as if hunting for a lost dog.

Our guests were bewildered and rightly so. Uncle Frederick was sitting in Father's place again, and I had begun to feel something like relief that perhaps finally she had put my father's defection behind us and was ready to live something like a normal person. Now I looked to Mim for guidance. She motioned for me to follow her.

"Please help yourselves and go on with the feast," she said smoothly, patting her son on the shoulders. "It's only natural that Huldah would be slightly confused. She has gone through a great shock this past year. Wren and I will see to her, and we will all be back in merry spirits momentarily."

Mim and I went into the yard, where Mother was tromping among the remnants of her garden, looking impatient.

"I declare, your father can never seem to find his way home to a proper meal." She clucked her tongue. "And your brothers? I don't know what I'll do. They must have finished that airplane, and they've taken off into the sky."

Mim went to Mother and grabbed her forearms. "Listen to me, Huldah. Your husband has been gone these many years. He's gone. He's left you, dear, and your sons died in the epidemic. They passed away and are resting with their heavenly Father now."

Mother looked at Mim as if she were a stranger. "Who are you to say such things to me? Surely you joke about all this or have confused me with someone else. Who can withstand such a tragedy as you describe?" An emptiness came into Mother's eyes, a frightening blankness that I had never seen before, followed by a threatening blackness in her eyes, as if the bottom had fallen out of her soul. She shook Mim away.

"'Woe unto them that call evil good, and good evil; that put darkness for light, and light for darkness; that put bitter for sweet, and sweet for bitter!'" Mother backed away. I noticed our guests had gathered on the back porch. I was embarrassed, angry, confused—I didn't know what to do. Mim wasn't helping, either; I think she was as perplexed as I. If we could have thrown a sheet over Mother, tied her up, and hidden her in the hayloft, I think we would have done it right then.

Odessa and Pandora, hearing Scripture, apparently thought this was an appropriate time to trot out a Christmas tune, although the Christmas spirit was diminishing by the second. I had heard them sing it on many Yuletides before. It was their homegrown version of "Mary Had a Little Lamb."

> The lamb been born to a virgin girl,
> That lamb gonna free my soul.
> The lamb been born to a virgin girl,
> That lamb gonna free my soul.
>
> The lamb got born in a manger cold,
> That lamb gonna free my soul.
> The lamb was born for a sinnin' world,
> That lamb gonna free my soul.

Mother's eyes sparkled, and she went to the sisters; she startled them by kissing each one on the cheek, and then she looked at the assembly on the porch. "My, I've gone and gotten you all away from the table. Everything will be growing cold. We've still got dessert—pecan pie, sweet potato pie, fruitcakes I made back in September that should be just delectable now."

161

She went inside, followed by the rest. Uncle Frederick came down and whispered in my ear, "I think it might be wise if I stayed on for a few weeks, if you'll have me."

I looked into his eyes and into Mim's, knowing they could see my tears. I wished I could tell them what was in my heart, what was happening to me, and how badly I needed them both. But I couldn't tell them today. I could only think of two things to say.

"Thank you, Uncle Frederick." I kissed him and allowed him to put his arms around me. For a moment I, too, felt that my father was back. "Merry Christmas."

11

THE ONE TRUE THING

So Uncle Frederick became a new fixture in our household, taking over the farms and hard work that I had become less able to do as time passed. I was forced to reveal my secret to him, because soon I began to show, and I couldn't explain it away by telling him that I was simply growing fat. He took it with more fortitude than anyone could have expected. I suspect he had seen much in his life, and it took much more to shock him than the rest of us.

Soon the others knew as well. Mim guessed, and Uncle Frederick took it upon himself to tell Miss Lanie, which angered me more than if Mother had blurted the news. I felt ashamed. If I could have hidden it from her forever, I would have. Like Mother, Miss Lanie had high expectations for me, and now those expectations and dreams were like dust particles, invisible unless exposed to light.

When she came to see me, I turned away from her, too brokenhearted to face her.

"Wren, dear, this is no cause for shame," she said, putting her hands gently on my shoulders and turning me around. "A crime was committed. Had you come to me I would have rousted out the sheriff and we would have put Skeeter Lowe underneath the jail."

"I couldn't tell you. It was my fault. I went with him because I wanted to learn how to drive the car." The tears came then, tears I had cried in secret for months, tears I was relieved to shed in the open. Miss Lanie pulled me to her and hugged me.

"You cannot blame yourself. You have seen all the terrible things that can happen to people through no fault of their own," she whispered as my tears soaked into her woolen coat. "So don't dwell on what he did to you. He's gone now, and he can never hurt you again."

I pulled away. "Mother wants me to give the baby away."

She extracted a lace hanky from her purse. "And what do you want to do?"

"I want to keep the baby. The baby's mine, and I love it," I said between sniffles. "She's being cruel and insufferable like she always is. I won't let her do it."

"Then we will see that it doesn't happen."

So I took Miss Lanie's word for it. I was relieved that the secret was out, if only in a limited circle. At least I could deal with it openly; to a few, the truth reprieved me from having to explain myself.

For her part, Mother went on as if her outburst had never occurred. Uncle Frederick could see that she was unbalanced. So could Mim, but no one in the family had ever been sent away. We were the type of people who took care of our own. None of us wished to put her in a place where she might fare worse than she would under our watchful care. On most days, she behaved in what most people would think a normal manner, except for the fact that she spoke to an absent husband and searched for dead children across fields and behind haystacks. She still tended to business that needed tending to and looked after me better than she had the boys. We decided to bear it.

Thracia returned a few days after Christmas, just as mysteriously as she had disappeared. Of course, no explanation would be forthcoming, unless she could communicate through hieroglyphics or smoke signals. I tried to convince her that we didn't need her and that she could go back to wherever it was she had come from, but she seemed convinced that it was her duty to see me through those gravid months. There was no dissuading her.

So I adopted her as a mystery that needed solving. As I was relieved of responsibilities one by one, I found that I had little to do other than read or think, so I began studying Thracia.

Her face had a familiarity I couldn't trace. I studied its shape, the color of her skin, the blackness of her hair and eyes, the curves of her chin and cheeks, but I couldn't recollect whom she resembled. As I said before, I had never seen her with anyone in town. She was the most solitary person I had ever known. So I decided that turnabout was fair play. Instead of Thracia following and staring at me all the time, I decided I would follow her. Stare at her. Like all things, she seemed to accept this as another part of her life.

I discovered something else about Thracia. She was devious and mischievous. That girl turned out to be even more frustrating than I could have imagined.

For some reason, Thracia didn't trust Jake, nor vice versa. Whenever she went near him, he began to paw the ground and back away, tossing his head back and forth as if to say, "You're not taking me out." So she walked wherever she had to go. Mother hadn't prohibited me from walking—yet—so I began to follow Thracia whenever she left the property.

Following Thracia was like trying to follow a cat. She would walk along for a while, then suddenly stop and sit on the side of the road, staring into space while she munched an apple she had put into her coat pocket or sucked a piece of hard candy. Then she would rise again and veer off the road onto some side alley for a spell, then dodge into the woods and run away. Once I thought I heard her laughing. Perhaps I imagined it.

One day I just flat out asked her to show me where she went whenever she went into the woods, because although I often waited, she would never emerge where she had entered. I would always spot her later, walking down the road, her basket full of whatever it was she had gone to town for, heading back to our house, where she went on as if nothing were amiss.

Just once, I wanted to find out where she went, because she always seemed to enter the woods at the same spot each time. A couple of times I followed her in, but I became afraid of getting lost and stayed within eyeshot of the road. A clear path was not discernable, so I soon gave up.

Other intrigues also captured my attention, the greatest being Uncle Frederick's growing interest in Miss Lanie.

Mother did her best to discourage the relationship. Like Mim, she thought herself a matchmaker and thought that Miss Lanie and Dr. Redmond were immensely more suited to one another. However, Dr. Redmond seemed indifferent to Miss Lanie's adventurous nature, and Uncle Frederick was a magnet for her desire to see the world and experience all it had to offer. Once Uncle Frederick finished the day's chores, he became notably absent during the late afternoon and evening hours. I assumed that he was off courting my friend and champion.

I think Mother and I assumed it was just a distraction. Uncle Frederick had never married, had explained that marriage would only have slowed his business, which remained utmost in his mind. Telegraphs arrived daily from his West Coast agents asking for advice and orders on how to handle specific transactions. It was growing more apparent that he would soon have to leave before his business fell apart.

It was too bad that he had to tear apart the rest of my world in the process.

"Miss Lansdale has agreed to become my wife and accompany me home to San Francisco," he announced one evening. Miss Lanie stood at his side, beaming and fashionable as always in a new aubergine dress he had commissioned from Mrs. Cochrane especially for her.

I didn't know what to say. Mother gaped at them for a moment.

"Why, I think that is just wonderful," she finally replied. I think she saw this as an opportunity to extract me from Miss Lanie's influence—distance would take care of that—and marry off her brother in the bargain, so she and Mim could stop worrying about who was taking care of him out there in the wicked city. "You must have the wedding here. Mustn't they, Wren?"

I just nodded.

At that moment, it was as if the rest of my heart died. In a way, I was happy. Miss Lanie would no longer be just a friend—she would become my aunt, a relative by marriage, 'til death do us all part. I was also terrified. She was my one friend in this world, the one person who I felt truly loved me and respected me for who I was.

We would share no more afternoons of tea and poetry. No more discussions on the day's most pressing political topics. No more exchanging books and newspapers or simply walking the grounds of the academy, enjoying the weather and blooms of the seasons.

Once again, I had to pull myself together and make the best of things. Miss Lanie came to me. "Wren, you must be my maid of honor," she said, arranging my hair around my neck. "I'll have Mrs. Cochrane make you a glorious gown, as she is making one for me. We will adorn ourselves in splendor."

I had never seen her so happy. Uncle Frederick slid his arm around her slim waist. "I know this is hard for you, Wren, me taking away your best friend. If it's any comfort to you, I promise I'll take very good care of her. We both know how precious she is, as are you."

I plastered on a smile. "I'm happy for you both," I said, with as much dignity and belief as I could muster.

"I know someday, a good man, a Christian man, will come along who will see you for the wonderful woman that you are growing to be," Miss Lanie said, as Mother corralled Uncle Frederick and began inundating him with wedding plans.

Shaking my head, I tried to formulate a reply. "I don't know if that's possible."

"Anything is possible, Wren. I had nearly given up on finding love before your uncle arrived. So don't lose faith, in God, yourself, or anything else in this life, especially love. It is the one true thing of which we can all be sure."

Which brings me to Dr. Redmond.

As usual, he arrived in the wake of this new upheaval. He had discerned that I was with child. He *was* a physician first. When he came around offering to see me through my baby's nascence, Mother so thoroughly scolded him for his audacity that he was again left speechless.

"I will see to the birth of her child," Mother responded when he showed up at our door one morning, armed with a sheaf of government tracts detailing the latest guidelines for expectant mothers. "I do not need pamphlets and bulletins to tell me about the trials women have endured for thousands of years. I have been present at the births of many of the town's fine young citizens. I will see to Wren's as well."

"But she is your daughter," he responded, trying to draw himself into a dignified posture. "Obviously, this baby is the result of violent trauma."

He avoided my eyes even as I sought his.

He knew.

How could he have known? Could he have guessed? Could there be gossip circulating about me of which I was unaware?

Could Skeeter have told someone what he had done to me before he died?

I nearly died a death myself then. If Dr. Redmond knew, then surely others in the town knew. My suffragette tendencies came back to life then, and I decided to ask him straight out.

"How did you find out?" I fixed my eyes on his face, finding myself drawn to it in spite of my anger.

He shrugged, finally meeting my gaze with those jade eyes that nearly made me forget my vow to hate the male species for the remainder of my life. "I'm afraid there has been talk, Miss Birdsong. And I noticed certain symptoms when I was here at Christmas."

"Do you make all of your diagnoses based on non-physical examinations, Dr. Redmond?" Mother asked, arms akimbo, as if she was trying to increase her size and thus intimidate this man who was showing nothing but concern for my well-being.

"No, Mrs. Birdsong, that is why I'm here. I would like to help your daughter through this time, if you will let me."

"I won't," Mother said abruptly and turned to go into the house. "You may visit her as a friend, but you will not lay a hand on her in the medical sense. She *has* endured a trauma at the hands of an evil boy, and I will not let you amplify her grief. We women have tended to our own, and we will tend to her." She walked inside, letting the screen door slap shut behind her.

I swung back and forth on the swing, while Dr. Redmond took a seat on a porch rocker and put his hat on his knee. It was a chilly day, but the sun was bright. Mother had encouraged me to enjoy the fresh air, which I did, because it meant I didn't have to stay inside that empty house.

"Your mother is very protective," Dr. Redmond said, rocking, his head against the back of the chair.

"When she chooses to be," I replied, drawing my coat around my expanding belly. "I'm afraid she's trying to compensate."

"For what?"

"For her inattention to my brothers during the epidemic. She wasn't home for a single one of their deaths. She's trying to make up for it by ensuring that my baby is born alive. Then she plans to take it from me and give it away to strangers."

"I'm sure she only has your best interests at heart."

"She has never had my best interests at heart." I stood and faced away from him, watching the wind whip through the broom straw that covered the fields across the road. "I've never been much more than a servant to her and my brothers. Since Papa left, she's been a lunatic that I have to suffer on a daily basis as if nothing is wrong. She

THE ONE TRUE THING

won't even face the fact that he left her, that he left us all." Tears rolled down my cheeks, and I bowed my head so my hair would cover my face. Dr. Redmond stood next to me, bracing against the porch rail, watching the broom straw bend and sway.

"It is a rare individual whose parents have not wounded them in some way." His voice was quiet and strong, and his hand lay on the banister close to mine but not touching. His hands were fine and slender but strong. I longed to take one of them in mine, a thought that surprised me. I wanted his hands to caress my hair, to wipe the tears from my face, to reassure me that the hands of a man could do good, could wipe away the evil of hands that were soiled. Yet I was too afraid to make my desire known. I was afraid of making another mistake.

"You say that like someone who knows," I replied, turning now to face him, willing at least to let him see the tears coursing down my face. He reached into his pocket and brought out a fresh handkerchief, warm from being close to his body. I wiped my tears with it and put it into my own pocket.

"If I can't be your physician, then perhaps you would consent to my being your friend?"

The kindness of his smile enveloped me like a sun-warmed blanket. I no longer felt the chill of the day.

"I'd like that," I said, and as we whiled away the afternoon on the porch, I began to realize that men weren't the enemy after all.

My next obstacle was Mim. She summoned me to her small house one day in early February, where I was placed in the center of a circle and inspected by Odessa and Pandora as if I were some scientific experiment. Mother had advised me to stay home, certain that I was about to undergo some sort of ritual African motherhood rite, which would have been moot anyway, since Mother had no intention of allowing me to actually mother my child.

Instead, the sisters indoctrinated me with centuries of superstition concerning childbirth.

"You needs to get rid of them cats," Odessa began, rocking back and forth, sucking on a pipe that she held between her gums. I couldn't remember either of the women ever having teeth, and they resisted Mim's attempts to get them to a dentist.

"I love Titania and Tiberius," I replied. "They're a great comfort to me. They remind me of Micah. I read to them much as he did."

"Cats cain't understand no readin'," Pandora said, cackling. "I don't care how fancy they name is."

"Well, they're good listeners."

Mim huffed. "They'll suck the air out of a baby's mouth."

I glared at her. "The baby might not be there for them to even try, Mim. Mother's threatening to make me give the baby away."

"She will not. That baby has Lowe blood. I'll see to it that the blood remains in the family."

I couldn't believe what I was hearing. It took several moments to formulate a reply. She knew the circumstances of how I had come to carry Skeeter's child, although I tried not to think of it as such. It was typical for Mim to think more about the social implications rather than the effects such a trauma would have had on my spirit.

"That makes no sense. I can't reveal who the father of this baby is; I'd be too ashamed."

"Chances are, people already know. Bethel Creek is a small town. People talk," she said, leaning forward in her rocker. "I'm certain the Lowes would not want to lose their only grandchild to strangers. In fact, if I cannot convince your mother to let you keep the child, perhaps they would agree to adopt it."

Mim had that self-satisfied look she got when she sensed she was gaining some control over a situation.

"Don't let nothin' skeer you," Odessa interjected, oblivious to the exchange. "You looks at pretty things 'cause what you sees whilst you with child can cause you to get a ugly baby."

"Don't took it to no cotton field," said Pandora.

"Mmmm, mmmm," Odessa agreed.

"Why not?" I asked, keeping my eyes on Mim.

"'Cause it'll grow up to pick cotton. Baby from a Birdsong and a Lowe be's too fine to pick cotton."

Even the old women were conscious of this baby's ancestral status.

"Do none of you even care that this child is a child born of violence and that I want it to have nothing to do with the Lowes?" I spoke in level tones in spite of my desire to scream until my ribs split. "This child is mine and mine alone."

"That baby be's God's child," said Odessa.

"Amen, sister," Pandora echoed.

"Wren isn't sure she believes in God right now." Mim fixed her sapphire eyes on mine, her hands folded in her lap as if she made such insightful pronouncements every day.

"If there were a God, he would not have allowed this to happen to me. I would not be having a child. Skeeter would not have attacked me. I would be a suffragette or a nurse saving soldiers at war. Anything besides being stuck here in Bethel Creek." I pulled my coat tighter around me, which was getting more difficult to do—my body was expanding at an amazing rate. The baby was quite active, often keeping me awake at night, causing the need for long naps during the day. Sleep was what I longed for now, sleep to escape the opinions and declarations of people who didn't know anything of what was really in my heart.

"You wants to know if it's a boy or a girl?"

Odessa's question stopped me short.

"You can tell that?"

"Some folks believes that if you's carrying it high or low, you can tell if it's one or t'other, but we gots us a different way. Can I borry your weddin' ring, Miz McRae?"

Mim took off her ring and handed it to Odessa, who went to her sewing basket and pulled out a spool of thread. She tied the string to the slim golden band, then instructed me to hold out my palm. I did while she held the makeshift pendulum over my hand. The ring began to swing in a circle while the three women watched grimly.

"What's wrong?" I asked, alarmed by their expressions. "Is something wrong with the baby?"

"No, chile," Pandora said. "You's gone have a baby gal."

A girl. "That's wonderful."

"No, it's not," declared Mim. "We need a boy to carry on the family name."

I could see why Mother didn't get along with Mim. "I'm sick of all this talk about family names and bloodlines and ancestry." Snatching the ring from Odessa, I took Mim's hand and slapped it into her palm. "Blood runs through the line of the mother as well as the father. This child will be mine. It will have my name, boy or girl. This child will be a Birdsong, not a Lowe. Don't you dare think otherwise."

I stomped from the little house and down the road. For once, the sisters didn't even have a song in reply.

In the beginning I hadn't wanted to become attached to the baby growing inside me. I reminded myself that its father was a monster, an evil man. Although I had given up on God, I still believed Satan was alive and well and had wreaked his havoc on my life. Still, as time wore on, and I felt the baby living, its tiny growing feet kicking against my belly, I knew that I couldn't *not* love the child. I could not cast blame on it for its own existence. The worst thing in the world anyone could do was to bring a child into the world and not love it, no matter their reasoning or how the child came into existence.

Maybe that was why Mother wanted to give it away. Perhaps she feared that I couldn't love it. Only I already did. I couldn't imagine placing it into another woman's arms, couldn't imagine not feeding it and holding it and kissing it and dressing it each day and putting it to bed each night. I felt the warmth of its body with mine, knowing I had been given something precious to protect.

Despite Mim's contentions, I was proud that this was my child, that this child was a Birdsong, first. Through its body coursed the blood of my father and mother and their parents before them, and so on. If I could have believed in grace at that moment, surely I carried it within my own body. I was determined that no one would take it away.

It was soon after that Uncle Frederick and Miss Lanie were married. I can't say it was the worst day of my life because I had endured so many worst days over the past few months that another could hardly find a place among them. It was not among the best days, though, because while I was gaining an aunt, I also felt as if I were losing my best friend.

175

They had to choose Valentine's Day. Mother and I festooned the house with red-and-white crepe paper and red hearts. Bowls of paper-whites that we had forced laced the house with their subtle fragrance. Thracia cooked the main part of the wedding feast, but Mother and I fussed over the wedding cake, managing to reproduce a two-tiered confection we had seen in an old magazine. It was a little lopsided, the way I was beginning to feel physically, but frosting, strategically applied, can cover a multitude of imperfections. Kind of the way Mother and I disguised the clefts in our relationship, and the broken spaces in our souls, so two people we loved could have their day of happiness.

Miss Lanie came over early, and as maid of honor I helped her into the exquisite white gown that Mrs. Cochrane had made, possibly her finest creation. The fitted bodice, the skirt that draped so elegantly, the pearl trim so painstakingly sewn by hand—each detail was a marvel. When I finished adjusting the veil, Miss Lanie turned to face the mirror. To my surprise, she began to cry.

"What's wrong?" I asked, confused. I had only seen Miss Lanie cry once before, when Mrs. Boissevain died. "Is something wrong with the dress? I'll run and get Mrs. Cochrane—there's still time."

She shook her head, drew a handkerchief from her purse, and perched on the edge of my bed. I worried that her dress would wrinkle and told her so, but she waved me off. "I just thought how I wished my dear mother could see me today."

I sat beside her and put my arm around her shoulders as she let out her suppressed grief. It is on the most remarkable days of our lives when we miss most those whose love has brought us to that day. I often thought about Papa, how I might never see him again, that he would never have a chance to walk me down the aisle and give me to the man who would truly love me for me, as he did. I knew it wasn't the same as Miss Lanie was feeling—her mother was dead, as was her father. She would have no second chances.

No words of comfort came to me—she had always been my solace, and I didn't know what to say. It turned out to be the right thing.

"Thank you, Wren," she said finally, drying her eyes, standing tall, and smoothing that lovely gown.

"For what? I didn't do anything but sit here like a lump."

"Sometimes we just need someone to sit with us in our grief instead of spouting out useless advice like Job's friends."

It was my turn to cry then. "I'm going to miss you so much. You're my only friend."

She hugged me. "Darling Wren, love surrounds you. It's just that sometimes people don't know exactly how to show it." She fussed with my hair, which we had pulled into a topknot. "Whatever you do, do not let what's happened to you make you bitter. Your heart is still the same underneath all the loss and hurt. Think of your child!" She put her hand on my expanding belly. "This may not have started in love, but it is the manifestation of a greater love."

I nodded, not wanting to launch a theological discussion, because the time for the wedding was almost here. We linked hands. "I'll never forget the things you've taught me."

"Wren, I have learned far more from you. There's no difference between being a teacher and a student. One learns just as much from the other."

Mother knocked on the door then and peeked inside. "The minister's here," she announced. "And Frederick's ready."

After she went downstairs, Miss Lanie and I both took deep breaths, then started to laugh.

"You know, I'm not quite sure I'm ready for you to call me Aunt Lanie," she said as we walked toward the stairs. "It sounds a little matronly."

"Well then, I'll just keep on calling you Miss Lanie," I replied. "I don't think I could ever call you anything else."

Downstairs, Miss Lanie and Uncle Frederick stood before the minister. I took my place beside her, and Dr. Redmond took his place beside my uncle. As the ceremony progressed, I wondered that two people, separated by so much distance, raised in such different circumstances, could find one another by chance. It was the greatest mystery in the world to me, how two people on the immensity of the Earth could find one another, find love, find happiness. They looked at each other in the way that only those who know one another's minds can look, can see, can feel.

I was aware that someone was watching me, only this time it wasn't Thracia.

Glancing at Dr. Redmond—Connell—an image flashed in my mind. A man in a fine dark suit, a woman in a beautiful lace-covered gown, and it wasn't the couple the minister was now pronouncing man and wife.

It was Connell and me. Because he was looking at me the way Uncle Frederick looked at Miss Lanie.

I only hoped he would have the patience to wait until I could return that warm and loving gaze. I had a feeling it might take a very long time.

12

THE TREE OF LIFE

It became an obsession. Mother searched every catalog, every book on arboriculture she could find, and asked everyone she knew that knew anything about the plant world.

"Have you heard of the tree of life?" she would ask.

"Yes, you mean the tree in the Bible," they would reply, folks being used to Mother's propensity for asking unusual questions, though usually on the subject of salvation.

"No, I mean the *real* tree of life," she would counter. "It flourished in the Garden of Eden, so it must surely exist somewhere on earth now."

She wrote to librarians, college professors, scientists, missionaries in equatorial Africa and the Orient, knowing replies could be months or even years away. It didn't matter. She had decided that this was her mission: to find and grow the tree of life.

And she was supposed to do it in Bethel Creek, South Carolina.

Her theory went something like this: When God banished Adam and Eve from the Garden of Eden, the tree of life still thrived, because the tree itself was blameless of sin. However, by the time the flood came, the garden must have been lost to humanity, and the earth was too new for archaeologists to go scraping around in the nooks and crannies. As the world's occupants became more depraved and immoral, God caused the flood, which wiped out all life, save that which God commanded Noah to place on the ark, that of all *flesh*. Her argument was that the Bible didn't say anything about taking trees onto the ark, just whatever plants were needed to feed all those people and wild animals.

In other words, God saved the trees.

Her proof of this was when Noah sent out the dove for a second look, the dove brought back "an olive leaf pluckt off." Therefore, there were still trees, and subsequently, the tree of life must still have a few seeds lying around.

So lay the foundation of Mother's quest. I didn't have the energy to argue.

As for Thracia, she sat in the corner each afternoon, knitting. I had no idea what she was trying to make, only that she fashioned endless rows of stitches with no foreseeable end. Like the earth at the beginning of the creation story, Thracia's knitting was without form and void.

It was also constant. When she wasn't doing household chores or staring aimlessly into space or disappearing into the woods, the sound of clacking needles filled the kitchen. She reminded me of Madame Defarge in *A Tale of Two Cities*. I became afraid that Thracia was stitching the story of my life, just as Mrs. Defarge worked the atrocities of the French Revolution into her knitting. With every cast, stitch, or purl, I imagined my life being marked and counted, stitch by stitch, row by row, that she would reveal one day as I faced an unforeseen guillotine. Her incessant clicking never, to my recollection, resulted in a finished garment. No socks, no afghans, no scarves. Which, I suppose, was only fitting, seeing as how our lives are never quite done up into whole cloth. I daresay that on the day of our death, few of us will go off into the hereafter saying we finished whatever it was we were put here to accomplish.

I tore my eyes away from Thracia and put them on Mother. She was getting that wild-eyed look again, and I wondered how soon she was going to start talking to Papa and the boys. It had been a while since she had invoked their presence. The time was coming due.

It was late March now. Tiny buds appeared on the azaleas and redbuds, and wild pink-and-white dogwoods began to blossom along the creek bank. It was nearly the time of year when Papa had left, and Mother always seemed a little more *off* when that time rolled around.

"Did you ever stop to realize that the Bible begins and ends in a garden?" she said, looking dreamily into space. Stacks of books covered the kitchen table. I sat across from Mother, eating a bowl of grits and collard greens, my daily ration that Thracia fixed for me every afternoon at 3:00, when my craving became unbearable. Mother had managed to grow the greens throughout the winter in a greenhouse constructed of old windows that Uncle Frederick had cobbled together, one of many projects he completed before he and Miss Lanie departed for their western destination.

"No, Mother, I hadn't thought of it." The food was especially good today, and I ate heartily.

She went to the window, staring out at the blank space where she would soon begin her new Garden of Eden. To my surprise, she had taken to calling it that herself. She had probably overheard me sometime when I hadn't realized she was listening. Micah and I had frequently discussed the content of her little plot, and we felt excluded whenever she rejected one of our suggestions for a new addition.

"Adam and Eve were placed in God's most beautiful place on earth, the Garden of Eden. They saw the tree of life—the first tree of life." She sighed. "It must have been exquisite. They could have lived there for eternity, had it not been for temptation. Had it not been for a fallen angel."

She turned from the window and returned to her volumes. "They fell from God's grace, as we all must."

"As we all *must?*" I had finished my food by now and pushed the bowl away. Titania and Tiberius wound around my legs, probably hoping for a morsel. Unfortunately, I wasn't prone to leaving any these days. "What kind of God is it who creates beings only to let them fall into sin?"

"It is part of life, child. It was to convince us of our need of his grace, his mercy, his guidance. We are born blameless, and before we are scarcely from the womb we eat of the tree of the knowledge of good and evil, and we are no better than Adam and Eve. Our sins mark us, and our place in the garden is denied.

"Then we die," she said, brightening in an odd way. "We return to the garden of paradise, where the tree lives. The tree of twelve fruits. 'In the midst of the street of it, and on either side of the river, was there the tree of life, which bare twelve manner of fruits, and yielded her fruit every month; and the leaves of the tree were for the healing of nations.'"

I didn't respond, having still discounted the Bible as hokum at that point. I didn't want to engage in theological arguments I couldn't win. Of course, winning any argument with Huldah McRae Birdsong was impossible. It simply couldn't happen.

Secretly, though, I was a little intrigued with the idea. I imagined seeing all my brothers again in heaven, standing with them around a tree of such magnificence, although I knew the tree was a figurative representation. Of what, who really knew. The Book of Revelation defies interpretation. It doesn't matter how many ancient languages one knows, it is a mystery, whether you believe in God or not.

"Mother, why is it so important that you find a real tree of life?"

She considered the question for a moment before opening one of her books. "I look at the Bible as a book of instructions. The good Lord placed everything here on earth that we would ever need to live. He placed the tree of life on earth. It is up to us to find it and plant one in our lives, in our gardens, a paltry substitute, so that when we see the one he has planted, the true tree of life, we will know God's true glory and grandeur."

Needles clacked. Pages rustled. The cats purred. Outside, the ground warmed with the approach of spring, and my mother was preparing to plant the tree of life.

But all I could think of was how to prevent her from taking away my child. I hoped that this new preoccupation would keep her from fixing her attentions on me. As long as she concentrated on her task, she tended to forget that I was expecting a baby and rarely mentioned my condition or what might happen after the birth. I suppose I was too optimistic, for her next actions showed she hadn't forgotten me at all—the one time I wished she would have.

She lifted her head from the book and rested her gaze on my expanding belly.

"It's been in front of us all the time, Wren," she said.

"What do you mean?"

"Your child. Your baby." She stood and came around the table and placed her hands on me. They were cold; I could feel their chill through my dress. "We have no one left to carry on the Birdsong name. Except your child."

"But it won't carry on the name, Mother; it's going to be a girl."

She straightened. "How do you know it's going to be a girl?"

"The sisters. They did a little trick with a—"

"A wedding ring. Child, child, child." She shook her head. "'But refuse profane and old wives' fables, and exercise thyself rather unto godliness.' I'm sure they filled your head full of foolishness and superstition. If only Mim would put a stop to it." She slammed her hands on the table.

"Your child will be a boy. It will grow to lead our family and preserve our family name."

I heaved myself from the bench and faced her. "What makes you think you know any more than the sisters? Do you know that you sound just like Mim, all this talk about preserving the family name?"

"'A good name is better than precious ointment,'" she quoted from Ecclesiastes, "'and the day of death than the day of one's birth.' Your child is the first branch."

"The first branch of what?"

"The tree of life. Our tree of life, the one that happenstance has pruned so maliciously, without regard to the future."

"This baby is no one's branch, or trunk, or limb, or anything else. It's a baby. It's my baby, nothing else."

"You will not give it away," she said, gaining strength and momentum. "But you will not keep it."

"If I can't give my baby away and you won't allow me to keep it, then who will raise it?"

"I will." She pressed her hands to her head. "I see it all so clearly now. All of this, all of your pain, all of this loss was for a reason."

"Reason? Mother, you're not making any sense." I began to cry. "I don't understand."

"I can no longer have children, and all my male children are gone. You are having this child to replace the ones that I lost. You are not having a child for yourself. You are having this child for me."

I backed away. Even Thracia stopped knitting and watched us openmouthed. The cats, sensing trouble, evaporated.

"Uncle Frederick!" I screamed, before realizing he was gone, back in San Francisco with Miss Lanie, importing and exporting and playing games with government inspectors. Who knew what he was doing, only that he wasn't doing it here where I needed him desperately. If there was ever a time to discuss putting Mother away, sending her to Bull Street in Columbia, now was the time to do it.

"Why are you calling Frederick?" she said, coming toward me as I continued to back away. "This is none of his concern. This is our private affair."

Turning, I ran from the house, as much as I could run carrying all the weight that I did.

"Don't run! You'll jar the infant," she yelled after me.

"You are not taking away my baby!" I ran into the barn, where I fumbled with the traces until I hooked up Jake, who seemed to sense my desperation. Mother ran in and tried to pull the reins from my hands, and I pushed her away. "Leave me alone."

"You are acting crazed."

I laughed, amazed. I couldn't help it.

"It's the pregnancy. It causes women to act strangely sometimes. This feeling will pass."

She was so calm that I stopped laughing and went on with my task. "Mother, if anyone is acting crazed now, it is you."

She stepped closer and grabbed my arm so hard I thought it might break. "How dare you speak disrespectfully to me. God has chosen us to fulfill a mission for him here on earth."

"I don't know what kind of God calls on someone to tear a child away from its mother for a selfish purpose that does no good for the child." Wrenching away, I finally got Jake buckled, got into the surrey, and shook the reins. "I don't know what's gotten into you. The voices you're hearing are not from God, Mother. It's a sad fact, but he doesn't exist. If he did, this wouldn't be happening."

With that I left, Mother's screams echoing in my ears.

I pulled onto the road and started toward town before I knew I had no idea where I was going. Then I realized whom I needed to see.

Dr. Redmond. He was the only one who could help. He had seen it happen before, how irrational she became, the delusions that wrapped themselves around her brilliant mind. A physician would know what to do.

So I pointed the surrey toward his office, heedless that I would be advertising to the town that I was indeed carrying a child. It didn't matter anymore—they probably already knew. Small towns are infamous for gossip; were it not for gossip, there would be no news, no word of who died, who was born, who was getting married, who had visitors or was going on a voyage. No one would know why marriages failed or people were shot or children ran away.

Jake traveled as fast as his aged legs would go. Poor animal. He was subject to all our tragedies, all our outbursts, and he didn't understand why we always seemed to be in poor humor. Yet the beast bore it all for some oats and hay and the occasional rubdown or pat on the nose.

As I passed Miss Lanie's school, which was shuttered and deserted, I mourned again the loss of my dear uncle and my beloved friend. The school was for sale, and no buyer had come forward. I so wished I could walk through its doors again, sit at the desks, or write on the boards. I wished I could learn from my teacher again, that I could erase the last year from my life. I thought of Uncle Frederick and Miss Lanie, of their happiness and joy; oh, how I wished it could spread, like a joy epidemic, into those of us whose hearts were broken and torn.

As for myself, I had given up hope of ever finding true love. Life was difficult enough on one's own, dealing with your own quirks and apprehensions and obsessions. Combine two hearts and souls, and one's existence became a veritable maelstrom of emotion.

Bringing a child into a relationship was something else altogether. Especially a child born out of wedlock. A child conceived through rape.

It would take an extraordinary man to deal with me, someone who could handle my intellect and my headstrong nature. I may have lost some of my dreams, but I hadn't wholly lost my ambition. He must love my child, accept the child as if it were of his own blood. He must be willing to become a true father to this baby, to love it and support it and cherish its very soul. I didn't see how finding such a man was possible.

It didn't occur to me that perhaps I was running right toward him.

I put those thoughts aside. Right now the problem was just keeping the child, much less finding someone to help me raise him. Or her. It didn't matter to me which it was. All I knew was that I had something of my own and wasn't about to let it go, not to Mother or anyone else.

Directly I arrived at Dr. Redmond's office. It was coming on late afternoon now, and the waiting room was empty. Tentatively, I called his name.

When he walked into the room, his shirtsleeves were rolled up to his elbows, and his hair gave him the appearance of having been blown through the vortex of a tornado. He looked so comical, and I had been so angry and tense that the sight caused me to burst out laughing.

"I'm glad to know that just seeing me brings you such joy," he said, a smile playing at the corners of his lips.

I laughed for several moments, then began to cry almost as vehemently. Sitting on a leather sofa, I buried my face in my hands. I could sense him sitting nearby, watching me in silence, until I collected myself enough to speak.

"Is it the baby? Do you need my help?" His voice was gentle and quiet, barely stirring the air between us.

"It's the baby, but not in the way that you think. Mother—" my voice choked; I didn't want to talk about it, but knew that I must—"Mother believes that I am having this child for her."

Dr. Redmond nodded. "To replace the ones she lost."

"How could you . . ."

"Figuring it out wasn't difficult, given her behavior at Christmas. I could see she was having a setback. Grief sometimes manifests itself in unusual ways."

I reached into my pocket and found the handkerchief he had given me. It was clean, and several times I had thought to give it back to him, but I found I needed it again. "She's only gotten worse over the years. Uncle Frederick and I discussed sending her to the state hospital, but I don't know that it would do any good."

"Hospitals are sometimes the worst places for the insane. The field of psychiatry is in its infancy. We know so little about what drives the human mind, what drives people to the brink of destroying themselves—and those they profess to love."

"Insane?" I had thought of Mother as disturbed and had even thought of her as crazy, in the sense that most folks use the word crazy. Yet insanity, to me, implied something much deeper. Something that we could never mend. Insanity seemed intractable, permanent. "Are you saying there's no help for her condition? That because she is my mother she has the right to take away my child?"

"On the contrary. If you can prove her insane in a court of law, then you would have a case to keep your child, although I'm sure many would agree with her that giving the child to someone with a proper home would give the child a greater chance at future success."

"My mother may be insane, but I most certainly am not, Dr. Redmond." I stood and walked toward the door. He put his hand on my arm.

He touched me.

I wrested my arm away and glared at him with every bit of hatred I could summon.

"Do not touch me," I said, keeping a couple of feet of space between us. "Do not ever touch me."

"Wren, I can help you if you'll let me." His voice was quiet but firm, his gaze locked with mine.

"No one has helped me so far. All anyone has done is offer opinions and superstitions and reasons why I'm not fit to raise this baby. I am not the one who's crazy." I started to cry, and when my voice came out again, I fear it was more of a scream. "This is not my fault. I didn't ask to have a child or have someone I thought I knew force himself on me and hurt me and take away parts of me I can't get back. I didn't ask to have a mother who can't understand why my father left and I don't know why he left and I don't know why my brothers all had to die, why Micah had to die, why they left me there alone with that crazy woman and my crazy grandmother and her crazy slave sisters and why my best friend fell in love with my uncle and my uncle fell in love with her and they both left me when I needed them to help me with Mother and I don't know why I don't believe in God anymore except that God died during a rainstorm and I don't even know why I'm here except I thought you could help me and even you don't think I'm fit to be a mother."

I ran out of breath. My heart was pounding in my chest so hard I thought all my blood was going to come exploding through the pores of my skin. Dr. Redmond walked across the room, picked up a wooden chair, and placed it behind me. I sat on the chair and cried for what seemed like hours. He sat at his desk, watching me. Once he bowed his head—I guess he was praying for me. Probably praying for God to show him what to do with this hysterical pregnant woman who had barged into his office and gone on a tirade about every bad thing that had ever happened to her.

We sat like that for a long time. Finally, I couldn't cry anymore. I was exhausted. My head hurt from clenching my jaws, and my fists ached, and my back and my legs felt as if the nerves were about to explode. I had never been so tired in my life.

Dr. Redmond saw that I had wound down. "Will you be all right if I leave you here for a little while?"

"You're not going to get Mother, are you?"

"No. I wouldn't do that to you."

I nodded. He unrolled his sleeves and put on his coat and hat before closing the door behind him. I sat in the fading light until he returned.

"Your grandmother knows where you are, and she will tell your mother," Dr. Redmond explained. "I have a room in the back here where you can stay the night. Mrs. Cochrane will be along shortly to stay with you. I think it's best we keep an eye on you."

I shot him a rueful smile. "Afraid I'm going crazy, too?"

"Far from it. We're just trying to keep the baby safe. You, too."

Mrs. Cochrane came directly, bearing a small suitcase containing one of her own voluminous nightgowns, which I donned. She tucked me into bed and stroked my hair until I fell asleep.

When I woke the next morning, she was still there. So was Dr. Redmond, who clearly hadn't slept at all, who seemed to know that I needed him as more than just a doctor, only I hadn't yet realized it.

13

THE CLEARING

Spring always made me feel as if I were rising from a deep, restful sleep. Birds singing joyfully, trees blooming with fragrance and color, the intense green of new leaves after a spring rain—these things had always brought gladness to my heart, making me feel that life was full of possibilities.

But this was the spring of 1919, and apprehension tempered my usual feelings.

Following my outburst, my circle drew close, becoming a posse of protectors. Dr. Redmond telegraphed Uncle Frederick and Miss Lanie, who subsequently bombarded me with a succession of packages containing gifts for the baby that she had purchased from fine San Francisco boutiques. The items—layettes, gowns, booties, bonnets—were dainty, delicate, elaborate with embroidery and smocking.

I had made a few items myself, but none approached the quality of handiwork in these pieces.

Mother fell eerily silent on the topic of my baby after that day. She would mention the coming birth in passing, ask about my appetite, or bring some small thing I craved—candy or fruit—or brush my hair, which had grown long and thick and prone to knots. She teased these out gently, trying not to tense my already aching back.

I didn't know who had spoken with her, and I didn't ask. I suspected it was Dr. Redmond, although I doubt she would have paid any heed to his advice. Mother listened to no one, except perhaps Uncle Frederick, and distance from that quarter ruled out any part in her change of attitude.

Still, it was all a little frightening. Everyone spoke to me as if I would be keeping the child and that Mother would not do anything to jeopardize that. I didn't know anything for sure, except that I was getting heavier and slower and more anxious by the day.

So was Titania.

The poor cat didn't have any idea what was happening to her, that she was growing fat with kitties and an appetite as voracious as mine. We would sit together on the porch, me threatening to break the arms from the chair, Titania trying to gather her expanding girth onto the narrow porch banister. She would sit contentedly in the afternoon sun, squinting her eyes, stirring only to hiss a warning at Tiberius to stay away. As her belly grew fat with the approaching litter, her gait became halting, and we spent our afternoons waddling around the yard until we tired and returned to our respective perches to await our time.

For her part, Thracia remained a presence, though not nearly as constant as before. She still snuck away, but I had given up all attempts to follow her. I still wanted to know where she went, and I lived in near desperation for want of this fact. Since I was past doing anything constructive, I spent many idle hours speculating on her life apart from our family.

Perhaps she came from some secret Indian tribe, one that the white men who settled our country had not eradicated or sent west. Perhaps she was a remnant of one of these lost tribes, an infant abandoned, raised by possums in the woods—which would account for her silence—only to emerge when she saw other beings who walked upright. Perhaps she was a gypsy who had run away from a caravan. Spinning these imaginary tales helped while away the hours and days.

Then I would think about the baby.

I began to wonder whom it would look like. I hoped it wouldn't look like Skeeter Lowe, or anyone in his family, and I had only recently begun to consider this possibility. Having a child the spitting image of my malefactor—the thought made me reconsider the possibility of giving the child away. Then I conducted a mental inventory, remembering the faces of my dear brothers. Charley and Jeremiah resembled Mother, Teddy and Wilson favored Papa, Nehemiah looked like a combination of Mother and Papa, and my dear Micah bore little resemblance to either, although most folks said he had a "family resemblance." I took after Papa's side of the family, as they say, although his family was long gone. Papa's family tended toward lankiness, and I had inherited his dark brown eyes and brown hair. My forehead was wide like his, and we shared a peculiar curve to our chins. Sometimes, as the years passed, I became afraid that I would forget what he looked like. The scant photographs we had of him had disappeared. Mother probably saw him daily in her mind, but she would not allow any of us to see even a small image of him in the flesh.

Holding my baby in my arms—the day I longed for was approaching. I intentionally cast aside any doubts and fears of who he—or she—would look like. My central fear was that Mother was pretending to be fine, that her plan was intact—her plan to make my child her own.

The thought made me livid. I wanted her to be a part of its life, to be its grandmother and dote on it the way grandmothers do. I did not want Mother to be this child's mother. *I* was the mother—not by choice but by right. It had not been my intention to bear a child out of wedlock, but I intended to overcome my situation.

On a sunny morning in late June, I went into the backyard and was amazed by the sight I beheld. Mother's new Garden of Eden was thriving, full of new plants and trees that were growing as if they had received a blessing from heaven itself. Mother had worked hard all spring, trying to bring her vision to life. I had kept a peripheral interest, noting her progress. It was only now that her efforts had begun to flourish enough to truly garner notice. I couldn't believe the change.

Growing biblical plants proved more difficult than Mother first suspected. Although our climate sometimes approached that of the Mediterranean, she was forced to substitute some plants for others.

Having designed the garden around cross-shaped paths, she had divided it into several sections, and a new stone fence enclosed the whole. Mother had a distant cousin who lived near the mountains, and she called on this cousin to have a number of stones of varying shapes and sizes shipped to her on the train. Several farm laborers built the fence right in the middle of spring planting, because Mother insisted it had to be done right then. They built it with much gnashing of teeth and smashing of fingers, which Mother and I were kept busy doctoring throughout the procedure.

That garden—it was a glorious creation. Rows of flowers and herbs marched in perfect order, and their fragrances filled the air. I stood at the crux of the paths and drank in the aromas, which varied according to the wind's direction.

When Mother had destroyed the garden the previous fall, she hadn't gone so far as to destroy all the trees. As winter waned, she had taken the time to add a few new saplings to the mix, some of which were substitutions for those mentioned in the Bible.

Fig and apple trees, the latter espaliered crosslike across the stone, sprouted new growth. An old friend who traveled frequently to the coast contributed a palmetto tree, which stood in proudly for the date palm, and the cypress tree hung precariously to life. She should have planted it closer to the creek where it could keep its roots wet, but Mother made a gallant effort to keep it alive on our bluff.

Oak and pine trees stood outside the wall, a short distance away, so the roots of the oak wouldn't uproot the stone fence. A boxwood substituted for laurel; the cedars of Lebanon could not have been a match for the fine specimen that stood guard over the south side of the garden. The locust tree spread its branches over the western side, shading the tender herbs that grew beneath.

We had quite a debate whether the Garden of Eden might have contained a chinaberry tree. With its mushroom shape, it provided a leafy umbrella of shade against the harsh sun; we spent many hours beneath its wide canopy as the days grew hot and still—Thracia and I sitting on one side of its gnarly trunk, Mother out of sight on the other side.

Oh—I had never seen herbs so lush. Mint, horseradish, chicory, parsley, fennel, garlic, marjoram, and dill overlaid neat rows. Staked vines heavy with gourds snaked among the herbs. Sugar cane and bamboo imitated reeds, and cattails mimicked rushes. Lilies and roses raised their tender buds to the sky, drinking in the rain and sun, turning their nourishment into rich colors.

A pomegranate tree overlooked this horticultural congregation. I ached to bite into a tart fruit, much as Eve must have ached for that fruit of the tree so temptingly offered up by the serpent. It was only fitting, I guessed. I did not consider myself a blatant sinner, but I saw no reason now to abstain from that which I wanted, within reason.

So it was that I stood there, intoxicated by assorted perfumes and blooms and textures, when Thracia sauntered by, holding something in her hands. The sun was very bright, and I thought perhaps I had been blinded, so I had to look twice to believe what I was seeing.

Thracia was holding a book. An open book. She appeared to be reading the book. *Reading.* It took a moment for this to sink in, for I had never seen her pick up so much as a magazine or a newspaper, even to look at the pictures.

She studied the book as she walked, seeming not to see me, which was unusual as I always seemed to be the focus of her attention when she was around. In fact, I had grown quite used to it and felt safe, knowing that at least one person had made my well-being her full-time occupation. In an odd way, I felt jealous.

Thracia was reading a book.

I began to follow her as she traversed the paths of the garden. She walked faster than I, and it was difficult to catch up, but I tried, because my curiosity now had me hard in its claws. Coming up behind her, I expected her to slap the book shut, as most of us do when we find someone is doing the visual equivalent of eavesdropping on our endeavor. She didn't do this, though, and continued to stare at the page.

I became frustrated. I couldn't focus on the words because of her movement. Finally, she stopped, and when she did, I came around her and snatched the book from her hands.

"Aha!" I exclaimed, closing the book and holding it over my head where she couldn't reach it. Thracia was nearly as tall as I, but her arms were shorter and try as she might, she couldn't get her hands on it. "I knew there was more to you than staring and cooking and sneaking off. I didn't know you could read!" I stepped backwards, to her frustration, because a look came onto her face I had never seen before—not that she had that many different expressions.

She became upset, and a noise emanated from her throat, a whine almost, and it made me feel sorry for her. I began to feel that I was taking a toy away from a child, and I brought my arms down, expecting Thracia to snatch the book back, but she didn't. When I began to examine the book, I believe my heart nearly stopped.

It was a volume bound in black leather, with good quality foil-edged paper. Embossed in gold on the front cover was the title *Walden, or Life in the Woods* followed by the name of the author, Henry David Thoreau.

I had seen the book before and had thumbed its well-worn pages as a child. I opened to a passage near the end and read:

However mean your life is, meet it and live it; do not shun it and call it hard names. It is not so bad as you are. It looks poorest when you are richest. The fault-finder will find faults even in paradise. Love your life, poor as it is. You may perhaps have some pleasant, thrilling, glorious hours, even in a poor-house. The setting sun is reflected from the windows of the alms-house as brightly as from the rich man's abode; the snow melts before its door as early in the spring. I do not see but a quiet mind may live as contentedly there, and have as cheering thoughts, as in a palace.

I skipped a few lines and read again:

Things do not change; we change. Sell your clothes and keep your thoughts. God will see that you do not want society. If I were confined to a corner of a garret all my days, like a spider, the world would be just as large to me while I had my thoughts about me.

The book belonged to my father, Mallon Birdsong. It was his favorite, and I hadn't seen it since he left.

Opening the book, I confirmed this identification. A printed bookplate inscribed *Ex Libris Birdsong* was pasted inside the front cover.

"Where did you get this?" I asked, my voice a whisper. The sun beat down on my head, and I felt almost faint, but I managed to focus my eyes on Thracia's.

Another look passed over her face. It was a look of knowing.

"You know where he is."

She didn't nod or shake her head, but I knew by her steady gaze that Thracia knew where my father was.

Thoreau's experiment of living a solitary life along Walden Pond had fascinated Papa. He had talked often about how self-sufficient Thoreau had become and how the brief respite revitalized the man, giving him insights into the human spirit that he could not obtain under the distractions of close living among his human neighbors.

"Take me to Papa," I said, grabbing Thracia by the arm. "You knew where he's been this whole time you've been living under our roof, and you never let me know anything about it. You owe me this!"

She pulled her arm away, the first act of defiance I had ever encountered in her. Folding her arms, she shut her eyes, becoming as still as a statue. I looked around to see if anyone was watching, but the place seemed deserted. I leaned close to her ear.

"You listen to me," I said, keeping my voice low anyway, on the off chance someone should make a sudden arrival. "I'm living here with a crazy woman who's threatening to take away my baby. Now I find out my father's living practically within earshot, only I don't know where, but you do. You've been keeping it from me. Now you either take me to him or get out of our house."

She opened her eyes, apparently considering the ultimatum. Living in our house was quite cozy, in spite of the ongoing melodrama, and I was sure she had grown accustomed to the comforts and steady.meals. Then she did something I couldn't have expected.

She held out her hand.

I stared at it a moment, then took it, and she led me toward the barn, where she proceeded to hook Jake up to the surrey. For the moment, they seemed to put aside their differences. Mother had taken to riding Pegasus, since I could not now even lift myself to the saddle, and she was gone. When Thracia finished, I got in, and she handed me the reins to me. I drove Jake to the road, where Thracia pointed the direction I should go. When we reached the point at the edge of the woods where she always disappeared, she motioned for me to stop. I did, and after I tied Jake to a tree, she took my hand again and we began walking through the woods.

The slim, serpentine path was clean and well cleared. I don't know how I had missed it before, although I'm sure Thracia had gone a different way just to throw me off. The path was long, and as we traveled deeper into the woods I began to feel a lightness, as if I were about to enter another world.

Soon, we came to a clearing. On the other side stood a cabin built of logs, overlooking the creek.

Beside the cabin stood the handsomest man I had ever seen.

Papa.

14

THE HERMITAGE

"Papa."

My voice had disappeared somewhere on that long walk; I could barely whisper the word.

We stood on opposite sides of the clearing for what seemed a decade before Papa laid down the ax he was holding and came to me. His brown eyes, eyes like mine, betrayed a sorrow I couldn't touch, and tears refused to fall across his face. Taking a last step forward, he held out his arms and I fell into them, where my tears drenched his shirt and his suspender left an impression on my cheek when I finally pulled away.

"My girl," he said, smoothing my hair away from my face and smiling. "You've no idea what a sight you are to me." He looked at my belly, tight against my dress. "I guess your time is getting close."

I shook my head. "I don't understand this, Papa. I don't understand any of this."

He led me into the cabin and indicated a simple chair, where I sat as he prepared a glass of cool water. I was amazed at what I saw.

Constructed in the spirit of Thoreau's cabin, the little structure was simple but functional. Four walls, a single room, divided into an area for sleeping, one for preparing food, another that sufficed as an impromptu parlor: Had this been my father's home for these past years? A small woodstove provided warmth and a place to cook. Two curtainless windows on the front, one on the back, overlooking the creek, let in the soft summer breeze. Tall pines and hardwoods shaded the cabin, keeping it cool in spite of the growing heat of summer.

Thracia entered and sat on a small pile of blankets in the corner, where she ate from a milk pan filled with blackberries. Purple juice ran down her chin, and she wiped it away with the back of her hand.

For my part, I sat in awe of this little cabin. So many questions filled my mind, I didn't know where to start. Now I was thrown into confusion, knowing that he hadn't gone far away as we had all imagined but was living so close to our home, in a place we could have gone if he hadn't wanted to come to us.

I studied Papa's face, smooth before but now bearing the lines that time engraves on us all, his hair, spotted with gray like a bird's egg. His hands were rough against mine, and we sat in silence for the longest time as my tears fell across this long-craved reunion.

When my feelings came together enough so I could think sensibly, I decided I would let him tell his story first. Then I would tell mine. Maybe together we could find a solution to both our dilemmas.

203

"How did you find this place?" I began, rubbing my palm against his.

He sighed and looked out the window, seeming to stare straight into the past.

"I've known about it since I was a boy," he said, pulling at his earlobe. "I used to come here and fish and hunt. My daddy showed it to me and told me that a man should always have a special place of his own, especially after he has a family and needs a little peace and quiet." He laughed softly. The sound was like a pillow beneath my swirling thoughts. "The quiet here is like a seduction to the soul. Once you've experienced it, you can't ever get it out of your head."

"So what did she do to drive you here?"

He blinked. "She?"

"Mother. What did she do? I know she must have done something, because you would never have abandoned us of your own accord."

He pulled away at the mention of the word *abandon*. I didn't know what other word to use. I'll admit that I did feel a deep hurt at what he had done, but somehow I couldn't blame him, going through what I had gone through with Mother.

"Wren, that's not what I intended. At least I never intended it to become permanent, as it has."

"Do you know all the boys are dead? Your sons?"

Papa walked to the window, where the tears he had held back streamed down the lines of his face. His shoulders shook, and I went to him, putting my hands on his shoulders while grief surged through his body. After a while, he dried his eyes with a handkerchief that had grown transparent from repeated washings and turned to face me again.

"If I could have saved them, I would have."

"But you knew they were sick."

"Yes. Mr. Hall, the banker, sent notes letting me know about the boys. Thracia brought the newspapers, too, and I saw the obituaries . . ." His voice caught. "I knew and didn't do anything to help them. I don't know that you or your mother or anyone else can forgive me for that. I don't even know that I can forgive myself."

This man, my father, was broken and lost. I loved him, but I felt angry and betrayed. I thought of all the questions that begged to be asked: *Why did you come here? What's Thracia's place in all this? Why is she living with us now and coming here to you? How does she know about this place?*

Papa took me by the hand and led me back to the chairs. He folded his hands and stared at the floor. "I need to tell you a little story. It's not a pleasant story, and it doesn't have a happy ending like the fairy tales I used to read you. But it's a story I hope you'll understand."

"Does anyone else know it?"

"Your mother knows some of it. Not all."

"Then don't tell me unless you can tell it all."

His eyes met mine, and he nodded. "Very well. You deserve that.

"When I was growing up, another family lived on our farm on the other side of Bethel Creek. I believe I took you there once, to show you a small part of your legacy."

"I remember. I remember the pecan grove and how I picked up those nuts for hours and hours until I couldn't feel my legs."

Papa laughed. "But they tasted good that winter, didn't they?" His eyes glimmered for a moment. "The farm was too much for Daddy. He needed help running it. The family that lived there was what we called mixed breeds—part Negro, part Indian, some white thrown in besides. Slave descendants, remnants of the Cherokee the government

205

hadn't sent west—we never really knew exactly what they were. Only that they were in need and they worked hard.

"This family was named Mills, and they had a daughter. Her name was Delilah." He shut his eyes and leaned back. "She was a beautiful girl, same age as me. Delilah and her brothers and me, we'd play together after our chores were done, and as we grew up, she became a beauty." He paused a moment, as if picturing her before him. "She was exotic and free, playful—being around Delilah was like drinking moonshine. Something about that girl made a boy lose his head. There should be a prohibition against such a being."

I sensed that he was becoming embarrassed by this divulgence, and I averted my eyes. My father was a man, after all, and prone to feelings often not easily expressed or understood by our sex.

"We became—close," he continued. "She had a child. My mother found out, and my parents forbade any further contact with Delilah—wouldn't even let me see the baby when it was born. Daddy put the whole family off the farm." He tapped his feet and leaned back in the chair.

"Then I met your mother."

"Did you love her?"

"Of course I loved—love—your mother."

"I meant Delilah."

He studied a honeysuckle vine that had curled over the windowsill. "I don't know that you would call it love, because we had little in common within our minds. It was a union of bodies, a union of desire. A union of sin, as your mother would call it. I guess you could say there's love of body and then there's love of soul. Sometimes you're fortunate enough to find both with the same person."

"Then Mother knew."

"Not until much later. Her father knew. He had delivered the child."

"Thracia."

Father nodded and looked at my half sister, who had leaned against the wall and fallen asleep.

"I married your mother—against Mim's wishes because she knew about the baby, too. The only reason she didn't tell your mother was she feared your mother would never find a suitable match on account of her unrestrained temperament. I reckon Mim was willing to settle for the likes of me in her daughter's life rather than have her go through life alone." He stopped, considering his thoughts. "Delilah and Thracia lived in different places around the county. I always managed to keep track. Then a few years ago, Delilah got sick with tuberculosis. It couldn't be treated, and she died not long after."

I gestured to the cabin. "Then how . . ."

"Delilah's parents were old and couldn't look after Thracia. The fact that she's a mute—well, I guess you've figured out how frustrating she can be to deal with."

I nodded. "It's like trying to speak with a tree sometimes."

"She knew a lot of things; her mother had taught her how to keep house and cook and such, but she was still a teenager. I didn't like the thought of her being on her own. So I was forced to tell your mother about her. Not everything. I didn't tell her the child was of mixed heritage, or who her mother was, even what her name was, mainly that she was a girl, a teenager. The fact that I had been with another woman before her was enough for your mother to vow that I should never lay another hand on her."

This last part didn't make sense to me. If Mother were so angry, why did she always act as if she were waiting for Papa to return at any moment? I asked my father the question that was on my mind.

"I imagine the knowledge that your husband has a secret child would be enough to throw any woman over the edge. I told her I had to go to my other child. There was no one else to look out for her. She told me that I had better not disgrace her in the eyes of the town." A bitter edge came into his voice. "I guess she's more like Mim than she would ever dare admit."

"So you came here. I saw Thracia with your copy of *Walden* today. That's why I made her bring me to you."

He smiled and watched Thracia sleeping. "Thracia hid the book from me. I suppose she got tired of seeing me with my nose stuck in it. I guess you could say I decided I needed to live more simply. I needed to make some kind of life for Thracia, since I was forced to neglect her for so long."

"Why is she mute?" I asked, watching her sleep so peacefully, the one person who knew everything but could say nothing.

"No one knows. As an infant she had a fever that defied Dr. McRae's treatments. That was probably the cause." Papa reached for my hand. "Wren, do you understand why I did this?"

I nodded. "A few months ago, I could never have understood a man abandoning one life for another." I put my free hand on my belly. "Now I understand it perfectly."

"It's a fine line between the right thing and the wrong thing, sometimes."

I looked at his hands and looked away, then looked back. Something familiar. A strong hand. A hand coming through an open door. A hand holding a rock.

"Oh, dear heaven," I whispered. "It was you. It was you who hit Skeeter on the head." I buried my face in my hands. "I thought it was Thracia, but now I know it was you."

"We were walking along the creek and took shelter under some trees to wait out the rain that day," he said. "We heard your screams." He began to cry. "If only I had done more. If only I had done it sooner."

"Papa, you probably stopped him from killing me. You couldn't have done anything else."

"I could have stayed home and suffered the consequences of my actions. Suffered your mother's temper, her pious condemnation of me. I could have lived in the barn if she wouldn't let me stay in the house. Leaving was the most difficult thing I ever did in my life." He clenched his fists. "If I had stayed, had been man enough to confront your mother and try to work it all out, at least I would have been there to protect you."

"You couldn't neglect Thracia any longer, just as I can't neglect this child I'm carrying. You may have gotten yours by choice, and I may have gotten mine by violence, but neither of us could help but love these children."

Papa took a deep breath and looked into my eyes. "I know I don't have any right to ask this of you, Wren. Do you think you can ever forgive me?"

Forgiveness. Accepting Papa's absence had been a struggle for us all, especially in the face of Mother's deteriorating mental state. Yes, I had been angry at Papa. How could I not be? He had walked away from us all, without explanation. But these last months, last years, with Mother, had given me a new perspective, an understanding of what he must have been up against. And after what I had been through myself—the violation, the loss, the grief, the constant worry and fear of what the next day would bring from Mother's convoluted, disturbed mind—I had to try to understand what it was that would make a man leave his family behind.

It came down to the fact that I had never stopped loving him. My father was human and prone to sin and mistakes, as was I and Mother and Mim and everyone else. That didn't give me the right to hate him or withhold my forgiveness.

I looked into my father's brown eyes and knew he was my last hope for help now. I had no one else left. I had no other choice if I wanted to be able to live with myself.

"I know the choice you made was a hard one. But your heart was too good to have left us out of malice," I said, taking his face in my hands and kissing his rough cheek. "I forgive you."

Something about saying those words shook me, but I wasn't ready to acknowledge what it was. This was no accident, no coincidence. This was all of whole cloth, part of a grand purpose. A tearing apart, a cutting apart, a sewing back together in a new design. And it was time to start making a new pattern.

"Papa, I need your help."

"Wren—anything."

"I need you to come home. Come home with me."

He pulled away. "I don't know that it's possible."

"Anything is possible. Look at us, sitting here together now. We're alive. We're together. I was spared from death, you from death—your isolation probably saved you from the epidemic."

"I was afraid to send Thracia to stay with you, afraid that I would lose her, too. But I had to know that you were being cared for, that someone was looking after you to the exclusion of everybody else."

"She has, and to know that she is my flesh and blood makes it more extraordinary. But Mother is trying to do to me what your parents did to you. She's trying to make me give up my baby."

"Give your child away? Wren, that can't happen."

"At first that was what she planned, that I give it away to strangers. Now she has it in her head that I should give it to her. To replace the boys. To replace you. To replace everything she's lost. She believes it's an idea from God, but I think Satan himself has hold of her."

He walked around the cabin, finally coming to the door and frowning out at the clearing. It was getting late. Long shadows fell across the yard, which had been swept clean with a broom, and the chickens pecked at the last bits of corn before going to their roosts for the evening.

"I don't know that my coming back will make any difference," he said quietly. "It might make her worse."

"She can't get much worse. We've already discussed sending her to the state hospital."

"You can't do that." He spun around, concerned now. "You can't send her away. She's never been away from Bethel Creek. Just the change would kill her."

"Then come back. Maybe your being there will make a difference. She might not say it, but she needs you. *I* need you."

"But will *she* forgive me? *Can* she forgive me?"

I didn't know and wouldn't say. All I knew was that she still loved him, in spite of what he did, and he still loved her. Fear was the thing that stood between them. I remembered hearing that perfect love drives out fear. If only they had given each other a chance then, instead of letting it all go. If only they would take a chance now as I had decided to do.

It was too much to fathom. I felt tired and heavy, and I didn't know if I could make it back through that narrow path in the woods. I leaned back in my chair, aware of a vague pain in my back.

Thracia stirred, then rose and went over to Papa, who kissed her on the forehead and hugged her. "Did you have a good nap?" he asked, much as you would ask a small child.

She nodded intensely, something I had never known her to do. Then she did something else I didn't expect.

Thracia came to me and smiled. Kissed me on the cheek. Then she hugged me so hard I thought the baby would pop out right then.

Which it apparently decided to do.

A sharp pain tore through my body, and I doubled over.

"Wren, what is it?" Papa rushed over and helped me to the bed.

"I hope some of Mother's medical know-how rubbed off on you," I said, clenching my teeth against the pang.

"You're not saying . . ."

"I'm saying I'm having a baby. And I'm fixing to have it right now."

15

RECLAIMED

Papa and Thracia watched me as if they were waiting on a cow to calve. You'd think they would have picked up something by being around Mother, but if they had it wasn't showing.

Papa sat near me, patting my forehead with a wet cloth and sending Thracia back and forth to the creek for fresh buckets of cool water. Yet as the pains came closer and closer together and no baby was forthcoming, we all started to get worried.

And despite two other people in the room, I felt very alone.

I was having a baby.

A real live, human, breathing baby that was going to be totally dependent on a girl barely out of high school, with no husband in sight, a deranged woman for a mother, a

213

mute for a sister, a father who didn't know his own mind about coming or going. A girl who'd lost all her brothers in the space of a year and watched her best friend get married and move all the way across the country. A girl with a grandmother who relied on the advice and care of two ex-slaves, whose way of addressing the problems of the world was to frighten them with superstitions, then sing them a spiritual. If they had been there, I expect they would have dredged up an appropriate selection to accompany childbirth.

Unfortunately, no one who knew anything was anywhere close.

I grabbed onto a twisted bedsheet that Papa made for me to hold after my fingernails had dug ruts in his hands. It felt as if the baby was trying to turn me inside out.

"Papa!" I screamed, every time another series of contractions began. "Wren!" he yelled back each time, unsuccessfully trying to lighten my falling mood.

I didn't know what to do. I needed Mother, her experience, her expertise, her love for me that I knew existed under all the madness. I thought about Dr. Redmond, my friend, who had offered to be my physician. I didn't know who could help me most at this point.

Grabbing at Papa, I tried to speak, but my voice was hoarse from all the screaming. It was deep into the night now, and the cabin was lit only by an old kerosene lamp with a dirt-streaked globe.

"Dear Lord," I found myself praying, the words feeling strange after my months of doubt. "Show me what to do. I don't know who to send for. If I send for Mother, she's going to take the baby away. If I send for Dr. Redmond, I feel like I'd be trading my friend for a doctor, and I need his friendship now more than ever."

I looked up at Papa, at his face full of love, and wondered how he could have left us all, if not for Thracia standing there, so competent in some ways and so needful in others. I could not have abandoned a child like her myself. Any child, for that matter.

If I send for Mother, she's going to find out the truth, I thought, not daring to imagine Mother's reaction to discovering Papa and Thracia's relationship.

I have chosen the way of truth: thy judgments have I laid before me.

The words of the psalmist gave me my answer.

"Papa, you have to send Thracia for Mother."

He shook his head. "I can't do that. We'll get this baby into the world, Wren. Don't you worry."

"I am worried. That's why I need you to get Mother. You can't do this alone, and I can't do it." I gritted my teeth against the agony that coursed through my body. "It's time for the truth, Papa. It's time for my baby to be born and the truth along with it."

He massaged my arm as Thracia came in with another bucket of water. Then he went to the table and, taking a tablet and pencil, wrote a note. He folded it, gave it to Thracia, then whispered something. She disappeared into the darkness.

I laid back on the pillows and blankets he had piled behind my back. The pain passed for the moment, but I was too scared to think about the baby coming. I hoped it would wait until Mother came. Right then, I wished it wasn't coming at all.

"I'm scared, Papa."

"Your mother gave birth to seven of you . . ."

"I'm not talking about having the baby. That's the lot of a woman, and I'm reconciled to the pain. I'm afraid I won't be a good mother. What if I go mad like Mother?

215

What kind of mother is that to a helpless child? Or even a grown child like me?"

I could see him searching for some wisdom to give to me, but it was slow coming. Not having been around us for a long time, and having to deal with Thracia in a different way, I suppose his font of fatherly wisdom had been depleted, or at least stashed away, like old clothes in the attic.

"You won't go mad, sweetness. You have a pure heart of love, and that will carry you through the times when your mind will make you think you're losing your reason."

"I missed you, Papa."

The loneliness shone in his eyes. "You have no idea how much I missed you. How sorry I am that I had to leave."

Then the pains returned, and I began screaming again. Papa started watching the door, like he was waiting for the sheriff to arrive and put him on the chain gang.

After a while, I heard a voice outside—Mother's voice.

"I don't understand where you're taking me, girl. Out here in the woods in the middle of the night. I know who my patients are, and I have never been to this forsaken part of our county in my life. The person who sent you could have at least said who needed me and for what purpose or . . ."

She came through the door of the cabin. Saw me, writhing with the latest contraction.

Saw Papa, for the first time in years, since he had packed up and left because of a youthful impulsiveness that had nothing to do with her.

She stood there a long time, until it seemed her eyes would glaze over and she would become one of those marble statues whose eyes seem to follow you wherever you go.

"Mother!"

My scream broke her trance. She walked toward the bed and pushed Papa out of the way. He went over to the door with Thracia and folded his arms against his chest, probably to hide his shaking hands.

For her part, Mother became focused on the ordeal at hand. She ordered me to push.

I shook my head. "I can't. It hurts too bad."

"Wren Birdsong, if you don't push right now, we're going to have some serious problems here. Now push."

So I did, with everything I had. My head pounded, and it felt as if my teeth were going to shatter, but I pushed until I couldn't anymore and fell back on the bed.

Give the child to me.

"No, Mother, I'm not giving my baby to you."

"I haven't said anything here about you giving that baby to me. You're delirious, child."

Give the child to me.

I kept hearing a voice. It wasn't Mother's or Papa's, and I doubt that if Thracia were going to speak she would pick now to start.

Give the child to me.

"You can't have my baby. The baby's mine."

"Push, Wren, push." Mother stood at the end of the bed, urging me through the pain.

Give this child to me, Wren. You are my child. As you are mine, so should be the child of your body.

It was God who spoke to me, tearing down the walls of my unbelief. He wanted my child. In my pain, my delirium, I believed he wanted to take away my child, as my brothers had been taken away.

Give your child to me. Dedicate your child's life to me, and I will make you whole.

I remembered a verse from Sunday school: "But as many as received him, to them gave he power to become

217

the sons of God, even to them that believe on his name: Which were born, not of blood, nor of the will of the flesh, nor of the will of man, but of God."

My child's life. Could I give its spirit to the Holy Spirit, who could provide it more protection and love than I could ever dream of giving? Would I be willing to trust this baby to the Lord's protection until it became of an age when it could claim the Lord as Savior and protector?

Dear Lord, I want to believe. I want to believe what you say. How I wanted to believe that God had a special purpose for all this pain, this suffering, this life I was about to bring into this world torn apart.

"Wren, the baby's coming now. It's part of the way out. Just another minute, another push, and my baby will be here. The new branch of the tree of life will be here."

I looked helplessly at Papa. Mama had a gleam in her eyes that scared me half to death, but there was nothing else I could do. It was no time to argue. The baby had decided to come into this world, despite our dissensions, and I had to help it.

The pain was so bad. I threw back my head as tears burst from my eyes. I cried to God, knowing the time had come to submit to his will and reclaim my belief. "I dedicate this child to you, Lord," I prayed. "Please protect him from harm."

Then I let out a scream that pierced the night air and probably woke every wild animal in Bethel Creek. When I got through screaming, pushing, screaming, pushing—I heard another scream, a little quieter maybe. I'm not sure, because this one wasn't coming from my mouth.

It was coming from the mouth of the little baby boy that my mother was holding in her arms.

The little baby boy that she was looking at like it was her own child.

I was out of breath, drenched with sweat, but that child could not have been more precious in my sight had it been made of all the priceless gems on earth.

"Give him to me," I whispered. "I want to hold him."

"There'll be time enough later," Mother said, wiping the baby, turning away where I couldn't see its twisted little face, its closed eyes, its compact fists waving in the muggy air. "Rest, child, and I will care for this tiny one."

"Papa, make her give him to me."

"He has no standing in this matter," Mother said sharply, holding the baby close against her bosom and putting a palm out against him. He walked toward her in defiance.

"Woman, I will not allow you to separate our daughter from her child."

"You say that with such authority." Her face was set, and she stared at Thracia. "Is this your concubine? You left me and took up with this half-breed girl? She must have been a child when you brought her into your bed."

"It's not like that, Mother," I said, keeping a watchful eye on her, wondering if I had strength enough in my legs to stand. "You're not giving Papa a chance to explain."

"I need no explanation. It's clear what's gone on here. Your father was a slave to sin before he married me, fathered my children, and now he's been enslaved again."

"I'm nobody's slave," Papa countered. "I left you because Thracia needed me."

"It's obvious what she needed you for."

"Stop your filthy thoughts, Huldah. She's my daughter."

For a second, I thought Mother might spit in his face.

"Thracia is your daughter. You expect me to believe that?"

"Yes, I do. I might not have told you everything you needed to know about me, but I never intentionally lied to you. You never gave me the chance to tell you the whole truth."

She watched Thracia in a way I had never seen before. As if she were the prodigy of Satan. "This girl—she's the product of your sin?"

"Thracia is my daughter."

"She's a half-breed."

"She's my daughter. She's half sister to Wren."

"She is nothing to Wren."

"She is something to me, Mother." I managed to sit up on the side of the bed. My head spun, and I felt like I was coming down with the flu again, but I knew this time it was just exhaustion. "I feel connected to her. If she's a part of Papa, then she's a part of me, too. I won't disown her because of the circumstances of her birth."

Mother walked up to Thracia, who sensed Mother's wrath and backed away. "To think I let you live in my home, thinking you were my daughter's benefactor, because you saved her life."

"It was Papa who saved me," I said, hoping my defense would somehow sway her. It seemed to grow warmer in the cabin each moment, instead of cooler as it would toward dawn. They all wavered before me—Papa, Thracia, Mother. My family, all of the immediate family I had left. I felt the spirits of my brothers, almost imagined that I saw them there, the uncles to my baby boy, whom I rightfully should be naming at this moment. Instead, we were all arguing over sins of the past. "Papa hit Skeeter with the rock. Papa kept him from killing me."

The baby wailed, drowning out my words. I held my arms toward the child, but Mother refused to budge. "Please let me hold him," I said. "I want to see him, Mother."

"No." She moved toward the door. Papa went toward her. "You stay away from me." Then she turned to me with a chilling smile. "Thank you for giving me this tree of life. It's even more special because it is a boy child, to replace all the boys that have gone away from me. I hope you'll be happy in this den of sin."

Then she ran out the door.

I tried to stand. Perspiration rolled down my body. I felt so hot. "I've got to stop her," I said, as Papa and Thracia just stood there, frozen. "Go get my baby," I screamed, but they wouldn't move.

I made it off the bed and began walking toward the door, but the room began to spin, and the floor buckled. I thought we were having an earthquake, until everything went black and I felt myself falling, and I despaired that Mother had made good on her word. She had taken my child from me for good.

They called it childbirth fever. Many women died of it, even far into our new and progressive century.

I wasn't about to let it kill me. I had to get my son back.

My son. I rolled the words in my head during the delirious days that followed. Somehow Thracia and Papa transported me to Dr. Redmond's office, where he kept vigil over me in the small infirmary, ministering to my symptoms as best he could, praying over me when nothing else seemed to work.

I was aware of some things, just as I had been during my bout with influenza. That Mother had gone missing with the child, that Papa had called in the sheriff, and that Papa now moved openly among the townspeople. When Dr. Redmond was called away, Thracia was my nurse, her face open and smiling as she cared for me. It was as if my father's pronouncement that we were sisters had opened up her heart, and she could now express her love for me freely. I recognized that her previous reticence had probably been wrought out of fear, mainly of Mother, and the fact that she was in her father's home but not of it.

So I lay there, helpless, in despair. Mother had kidnapped my child, the child I had grown to love before it was born, the reason for my being.

No one seemed to know where she was. Searchers beat the woods, kept a vigil on our place and Mim's, even telegraphed Uncle Frederick and Miss Lanie to be on the alert for her possible arrival in San Francisco.

During this time, I fought for my life. I prayed to God—no, I pleaded with him—to spare me. I couldn't believe that he had brought me this far only to bring me home and leave my baby in the care of a madwoman, even if she was my own mother. I was in pain, and the fever was unbearable at times, and I thought that I was surely about to join my brothers in that long row of graves.

I guess the Lord had other plans for me. Finally, the fever receded. I was weak and thin, much as I had been after the epidemic. My soul, however, nurtured a ferocity that no one could touch. Although evil and illness had savaged my body, the Lord had resurrected my soul. God Almighty had given me a mission and a purpose. He had given me a child who would grow up to accomplish great things. I knew it deep down in the very marrow of my bones. I knew because God had promised, and God is the only one whose promises never fail.

Days turned into weeks, and soon Dr. Redmond deemed me well enough to return home. I dreaded the thought. Where the house had fallen silent before, I now expected it to have the stillness of a tomb. Another soul absent, and the new one missing along with her.

So surprise was the least of it when Thracia brought me back to the house, where my father had resumed his rightful place.

"I decided I didn't need to ask anyone's permission," he said, helping me from the surrey. "It's my home the same as it is yours, and if I want Thracia to live with us, she will. No matter what your mother says."

I grasped his lapels. "Please tell me they've found her. That they've found my baby."

He took my hands and kissed them. "I wish I could tell you yes, sweetness. I've looked everywhere, and so has the sheriff. No one seems to know where they've gone."

It was the height of summer, and the days were long, but now my heart felt as if it were enclosed in a shell of darkness found only on the deepest winter days. My child had been born in a shack in the woods, and I had not held him, not even for a second. For all that I had gotten back—my father, a newfound sister—I felt that I had finally lost everything. This past year, the pain, the loss, the constant grief tinged with the hope of holding a new life in my arms—it had all come to nothing. I fought to hold on to my so recently reclaimed faith, and it was a struggle to pray. But I did it, because only God could know what was in Mother's mind, and I knew God would be the one to bring them both home, or lead one of us to find them.

So our days became a vigil. The sheriff would come by. "No word," was his usual terse pronouncement. "We're keeping an eye out."

I knew I had to have hope in the face of this terrible mountain of torment. All things, good and bad, have their purpose. I remembered how badly I wanted to become a suffragette, so women could have the right to vote, and I remembered that there are greater causes that we must advocate, greater fights to win. Those fights usually involve the ones we love, the ones whose lives we are entrusted to guide and protect. God gives us mountains to climb so we can face the glory that stands at the summit.

Finally, dissatisfied with everyone's efforts, I realized that if I were ever to find my baby, I would have to find him myself.

16

FINDING THE LIGHT

Papa tried to discourage me, but I had already lost too much. I couldn't get my brothers back. I couldn't regain my innocence or bring back my mother's sanity. But I could find my baby boy. And I was going to find him if it was the last thing I ever accomplished on this earth.

"Wren, she could be anywhere, she could have gotten on a train and gone almost anywhere," he said as I saddled Pegasus. The horse was clearly ready for an adventure, having been cooped up so much while I recuperated from my various illnesses and maladies, save for the few times Mother took him out. "You ought to let me go with you."

"Papa, you need to take care of things here. Keep an eye on Thracia."

"You know good and well I don't have to keep an eye on Thracia anymore."

Thracia leaned against the stall, grinning now. I grinned back.

"Do it for me. I've finally got a sister."

I mounted the horse, and he pranced around the yard for a few moments, excited that we were together again, seeming to sense we were about to embark on an important mission. "I know one thing you can do."

"What's that?" he asked, his arm around Thracia's shoulders.

"You can pray for me."

He patted my leg. "That's something I've been doing all along."

So I set out. Pegasus was an eager partner in my endeavor, taking me down back roads, exploring places I never knew existed until then. Somehow, I had lost all my fear of the unknown. It seemed that everything bad that could happen to me had already happened, that nothing worse could befall me. I had regained my sense of adventure, but now it had an urgency I'd never felt before.

Mother believed that by taking my child, she would somehow replace all the people she had lost or driven away. I was determined that she would not take my child for hers, but neither would I let her drive me away, as she had done Papa. I loved her, for all her faults. I forgave her in advance, because she was sick and needed help, help that Papa and I couldn't give, since we didn't know how.

I had already spoken to Dr. Redmond. He had arranged to commit her to the state hospital, if she was found. Perhaps with proper treatment, she could be relieved of her delusions. She could find her way back to sanity, back to the true faith, back to letting us love her, rather than trying to find her way through possessing another.

As I rode and searched, I prayed for guidance, that the Lord from whom I had strayed would not stray from me. I realized that while we can run from God, he is always there, waiting for us to return to him. Sometimes he seeks us out, but often he waits, in his perfect time, for us to seek him, to come back to his love, his mercies, his gentle correction. God had watched over me, and I prayed that he would watch over my mother in her darkness, over my baby with his light.

So it was that a light led me to them.

Pegasus's earlier enthusiasm waned as the trees began casting long shadows across the road. I was near Miss Lanie's school, which was still shuttered and closed. I rode up the lane, where I got off my weary horse and led it to the pump and brought up some cool water for him and myself. Sitting on the edge of the well, I looked around at the deserted property, wondering if anyone would ever take it over. The property was still for sale; Miss Lanie had left it in the hands of a capable attorney. However, a buyer was yet to come forward.

I thought about my days as a student, how I so loved learning and expanding my knowledge of the world. I still had some hope that I might someday return to school, perhaps to college. All that would have to be far in the future. I had other concerns, more pressing responsibilities.

"You ready to go home?" I looked at my horse, so faithful in his ignorance of worldly disappointments and troubles. "It's been a long day. We'll try again tomorrow."

I took one last look at the old school, when something caught my eye.

A light.

It was just a glint. Most of the windows were shuttered, but a few on the side and back had simply been boarded over. I noticed that some boards were missing, and I wondered if a vagrant had taken refuge in a deserted classroom.

Leaving Pegasus tied to the well, I went closer to investigate, standing on an old wooden crate that I found in the yard. I peered over the windowsill and discovered that the window itself was open.

Upended desks strewed the room. Chalk dust and cobwebs lurked in the corners. The brilliant colors of the state and national flags had faded from exposure to the sun; that was evident even in the dim light.

In the midst of this mess stood my mother, holding my precious baby in her arms.

Mother didn't seem to hear me grunt as I hoisted myself over the splintery windowsill. I righted myself and began walking quietly toward her. The baby was asleep, and I didn't want to startle him or Mother.

But she was ahead of me.

"I see you finally found us," said Mother, keeping her eyes on the baby.

"You're very clever, staying here where no one would think to look." I walked closer, and she didn't try to stop me.

For the first time, I saw my baby's face.

It was as if heaven had opened up its gates. If I thought I had loved the child as it grew inside me, and then more when it was born, it was only now that I knew the true meaning of a mother's love. I saw the being who had been given to me in such an awful way but who was innocent of his origins and faultless in his existence. I prayed then with a thankfulness I had never felt before.

He was so small—it was obvious he hadn't had enough to eat. I had wondered how Mother was nourishing this child and tending to its needs. Obviously, she hadn't been completely successful.

As for Mother, she was filthy. I had never seen her look that way. Her hair was loose and flew in every direction, giving her an appearance to match the disarray of her mind and thoughts. She appeared malnourished as well. I noticed a few pieces of fruit, some crackers, a pan of milk, a couple of baby bottles—I could only guess that she had filched food from barns and houses when the owners weren't about.

I approached her cautiously. The light in the room was dim; a couple of candles burned on the desks.

"Mother, it's time for you and the baby to come home." Dr. Redmond had warned me that if she were found, allowing her to maintain her delusion for a while longer would be best, until I could separate her from the child. "I think you need a clean dress, and that baby needs something to eat."

She rocked my baby back and forth in her arms, eyes still locked on its peaceful face. "I must look a mess. Mim would be soundly disappointed in my disheveled state."

Good. She knows she's dirty. Let me see what else she knows.

"Have you forgotten me, Mother? Do you remember that I need you to take care of me, too?"

"All of my children died except one," she said. "All of my sons died, and my husband left me, a long time before that. You're the only one left."

I hid my shock. She had finally used the word *died*. She knew they were gone forever.

"I'm sure you must hate me now," she said.

The statement stunned me. "I could never hate you," I replied quietly. "You're my mother. I'll always love you, no matter what."

The sadness on her face was so great. I understood then the reason for everything she had done.

Love is complicated, when it should be simple. Mother had loved us all, but she couldn't bear loss. It was hard

229

enough when she lost a patient—to watch the children she had borne and raised die, one by one, with no way to stop the inevitable—it must have torn her heart apart. All I could see was her apparent dissociation from the tragedies in our family. In her mind, she was sparing us the pain of seeing the loss through her eyes. Her revered father, the one who understood her aspirations, died, leaving her with a mother who didn't understand her at all and tried to make her into an image of herself. Her husband had made a painful choice, and by making that choice, left her without the man who loved her in spite of all her flaws. A vicious epidemic took her children, leaving her without their company and unconditional love. Perhaps that was what she feared most—that no one would love her. Or maybe she didn't want anyone to love her because she believed that was the loss that harmed her most.

I knew I couldn't commit her to the hospital. Dr. Redmond, Papa, and I would have to find a way to deal with her ourselves. The first step was to make sure she knew that we loved her and that we wouldn't leave her.

"I love you, Mother. I never left you, and I never will."

"But the Lord provides in our time of want," she continued. "He has promised us a tree of life."

"I know, Mother. It's wonderful. 'The fruit of the righteous is a tree of life.'"

"'And he that winneth souls is wise,'" she finished, sitting in a chair, her long, blond hair falling down around her face. Her eyes cut back and forth as if she were reading the Scripture. "'Hope deferred maketh the heart sick.'"

"'But when the desire cometh, it is a tree of life,'" I completed, sitting next to her, knowing that my own desire was just a foot away.

Tears covered her face, and I could see that she was tired, weary from her own ordeal, weary from the fight with her own demons and desires, those aspirations she had yearned to fulfill but had been thwarted through the expectations of her mother and our large family, and her inability to forgive and accept, when doing so would have been best for her.

"May I hold the baby?" I asked.

She paused a second, holding the baby's fist, kissing its downy head.

"Does he have a name?"

She looked at me then, tilting her face as if she were looking at me for the first time, as if I had just been born into her world.

"I didn't give him a name. Isn't that odd?"

"So what do you call him?" I said, as she finally did the thing that I longed for, the thing she knew was right. She laid him gently in my arms.

"I call him blessed."

We sat in the dark for a long time, as the candles flickered and spiked, while she cried and rocked. The baby slept on in peace. His little world was far from perfect, and so were the people who surrounded him. Maybe he knew in his tiny heart that he rested in his true mother's arms. Maybe he felt the grace of his true Father in heaven.

Maybe he just knew we loved him, from first to last, that we would always take care of him, and would never leave him, and those were the things that counted.

EPILOGUE

A flurry of last-minute activity filled the streets of Bethel Creek as its citizens waited expectantly for the swearing in to begin. It was early January 1973, and the town had elected a new mayor, at the same time making history in their small corner of the world. A cacophony of tubas and drums and trumpets and clarinets filled the air as the marching band began their tune-up, while visiting dignitaries scribbled changes on their hastily written speeches.

A few blocks away, in the old Methodist cemetery, a woman and her grown son knelt before a row of small tombstones backed by a larger one, which was inscribed with the name "Birdsong." A spreading tree, adorned with birds and delicate flowers, was etched into the stone. The two prayed together silently, as the woman's husband, the man's wife and children, and an elderly aunt waited nearby. After a few minutes, the woman rose, and she felt a little catch in her knee. Her son put a hand under her elbow as she slowly straightened.

"I guess it's a good thing I've still got my mind, because my body would never have gotten me elected," she said, laughing.

It was hard to believe how far she had come. All those years running the Lansdale Academy, first for girls, now a coed school that accepted students from throughout the southeast. Raising her son, helping her husband with his medical practice, advocating the causes she believed in—help for the mentally ill and their families, services for victims of rape, immunization projects—these activities had filled her life and fulfilled many of her aspirations.

Her son watched as she kissed her husband on the cheek. His father—he had never known any other—had loved him and taught him so much. Now that he ran the academy, he found himself frequently calling on both his parents for their advice and direction, just as he had done while raising his sons and daughters.

Wren Birdsong Redmond took Dr. Redmond's arm as the family formed a small procession to the gazebo. The man watched his mother, proud of all her accomplishments, thrilled that she had finally fulfilled her lifelong dream of holding public office, as she was now about to be sworn in as the first woman mayor of Bethel Creek. When he had brought her the newspaper that morning, she had read the headline and hugged the paper, crying and laughing all at once. He saw in her the young suffragette whose handwritten memoir he had stayed up all night reading, whose story explained so much about the remarkable woman she had become, the wonderful mother she had been to him.

Looking around the cemetery, he felt the past rise to lift him up. He knew the struggles of these people, the lives they had led, the tragedies they had endured, the joys they had shared. His was a legacy of faith and perseverance, a legacy he tried to share with his own children, and hoped someday to share with his grandchildren.

A shout came from the cemetery gate. He turned to see his wife and children waiting expectantly, his father looking bemused, his aunt staring, and his mother standing on the sidewalk, arms akimbo, her purse flapping in the breeze.

"Adam Birdsong Redmond," she yelled. "Are you coming? You're going to miss one of the best moments of our lives."

"I'm coming, Madam Mayor," he hollered back, running to catch up. "I wouldn't miss it for the world."

Linda Dorrell began keeping journals at age sixteen in hopes of one day writing the Great American Novel. Her career took a few detours before publication of the critically acclaimed *True Believers* (2001) and reader-favorite, the mystery-suspense *Face to Face* (2003). She is a former journalist and public relations writer; her stories have been featured in *Southern Living, Ancestry,* and *Pee Dee Magazine.*

The Trees of Eden, her third stand-alone novel, continues her exploration of the topics that fascinate her: family relationships and dynamics, how long-held secrets affect those connections, and how big events in history affect people on an individual level.

Although she rarely keeps a journal now, she credits that process as helpful during her writing apprenticeship. "Journaling," she says, "taught me how to analyze characters, explore the emotional impact of daily life, and create a coherent narrative of experiences."

When she's not writing at her Effingham, South Carolina, home, Dorrell enjoys reading, exploring the Internet, bird-watching, stargazing, and dreaming up new characters for future novels.

She also delights in hearing from her readers. You can write to her by e-mail at Lindorrell@aol.com. Also, you can visit her web site at www.lindadorrell.com.

In writing *The Trees of Eden*, Linda Dorrell extensively researched the 1918 influenza epidemic in America. "Weaving historical events into a novel, without making it sound like a dry textbook or television documentary, is a challenge," she writes, "but one I relish.

"When I came up with the characters of Wren and Huldah Birdsong and decided to set the book during the 1918 influenza epidemic, I knew my research had to be solid in order for the book to be believable. What I didn't count on was finding so many other interesting historical tidbits to include within the narrative."

The Internet and good old-fashioned journalistic trail-following helped greatly in Dorrell's research. She found firsthand survivor accounts of the epidemic and many details about the home remedies Huldah and others in Bethel Creek concoct in order to deal with the illness.

One day, while researching the women's suffrage movement, Dorrell tells how she found a story about Inez Milholland Boissevain: "I knew I had found Wren and Miss Lanie's heroine of the cause."

Another day, Dorrell ran across a transcription of spirituals that the Works Progress Administration had compiled during the Great Depression. "When I saw that they had recorded the words in my own community of Effingham, South Carolina, I knew I had to incorporate them into the book," Dorrell says. "The former slave sisters became the mediums for these sacred songs. I was cheered, too, by the many sites dedicated to biblical gardens. I wished fervently that I would grow a green thumb, and a strong back, so I could plant my own. I had to have Huldah grow it instead. Sometimes novelists have to live vicariously through our characters."

Weaving all this history and fact into a novel has its rewards. Many folks will never pick up a history book but enjoy reading about historical events in a context they enjoy, portrayed by complex and interesting characters who engage them emotionally and spiritually. Dorrell's wish? "I hope readers will find this true in *The Trees of Eden.*"